"THE MEPHISTO WALTZ RECALLS ROSEMARY'S BABY, BUT I FOUND IT MORE SATISFYING. . . . Duncan Ely, an aging concert pianist, and his beautiful daughter befriend Myles Clarkson, a freelance writer who once aspired to the piano; Myles' wife watches with apprehension turning to terror as Myles comes more and more under Ely's domination, as their lives are increasingly manipulated—before Ely's death, and even more afterwards. . . . TERRIFYING, SHIVERY READING FOR A DARK NIGHT."

—Allan J. Hubin,
The New York Times Book Review

"The delightful horror and the satanic elements of *ROSEMARY'S BABY*, with the suspense carried on a more sinuously fluid prose style. . . . Read it at midnight and you can turn off the air conditioning."   —*Library Journal*

"Fred Mustard Stewart set out 'to scare and mystify my readers,' and he has done a masterful job."

—*San Francisco Examiner*

THE MEPHISTO WALTZ

A Novel

by FRED MUSTARD STEWART

A SIGNET BOOK from
NEW AMERICAN LIBRARY
TIMES MIRROR

Library of Congress Catalog Card Number: 69-17367

*This is an authorized reprint of a hardcover edition published
by Coward-McCann, Inc. The hardcover edition was published
on the same day in the Dominion of Canada by Longmans
Canada Limited, Toronto.*

 SIGNET TRADEMARK REG. U.S. PAT. OFF. AND FOREIGN COUNTRIES
REGISTERED TRADEMARK—MARCA REGISTRADA
HECHO EN CHICAGO, U.S.A.

SIGNET, SIGNET CLASSICS, SIGNETTE, MENTOR AND PLUME BOOKS
*are published by The New American Library, Inc.,
1301 Avenue of the Americas, New York, New York 10019*

FIRST PRINTING, MARCH, 1970

7 8 9 10 11 12 13 14 15

PRINTED IN THE UNITED STATES OF AMERICA

"Sempre piano, leggiero e fantastico. . . ."

—Tempo marking in the score
of the "Mephisto Waltz."

Part I

1

The call from Duncan Ely had come at eight o'clock on a Saturday morning, which was Paula Clarkson's morning to sleep. Mumbling groggily, she rolled over in the king-sized bed, switched off her control of their his-and-her electric blanket, and picked up the phone.

"Hello?"

"Myles Clarkson, please," said a deep voice that had a faint trace of an English accent.

"This is his wife," she yawned.

"I know that," snapped the voice. "May I speak to Mr. Clarkson? This is Duncan Ely."

"Oh." The name woke her up. "Just a moment, please."

Covering the mouthpiece, she rolled over and put her hand on her husband's naked shoulder.

"Myles, it's *him!*"

"Huh?"

"Wake up! It's Mr. Ely."

Myles Clarkson was not at his best in the morning. Rolling on his stomach, he pulled the blanket over his head. Paula tugged it off with her free hand.

"Myles, come *on!*"

Myles struggled to a sitting position, yawned and scratched his broad chest.

"Jesus, what time is it?"

"Eight."

"Great." He reached out and took the phone. "Hello?"

Myles, at thirty-two, didn't look a day older than he had when he'd met Paula nine years before at an unusually dull and drunken party on East Seventy-fourth Street. He was just out of the Navy then and just in the Juilliard, dreaming of a brilliant concert career and competing against the other enormously talented young pianists his age. Paula, fresh out of Middlebury, had thought he was good-looking and "interesting." Three dates later, she was convinced he was the most fantastic man she had ever met. Eight and a half years of marriage hadn't changed her mind.

"At nine o'clock?" Myles rolled his eyes. "Of course, Mr. Ely. No, I'm just finishing breakfast. I'll see you then."

He handed the phone to Paula and bolted out of the bed to the bathroom.

"Christ, he wants to see me at *nine!* Is he out of his mind?"

"I'll make coffee."

Paula threw on a bathrobe and hurried out of their small bedroom into the hall. Automatically she looked in on Abby, their seven-year-old daughter. She was sound asleep. Brushing her long, dull-blond hair back and wishing they had two bathrooms, Paula hurried up the stairs to their second-floor kitchen and put on the water.

Myles had been maneuvering three weeks to get the interview with Duncan Ely, who was notoriously hostile to reporters. The phone call was what they had been waiting for, and if Ely liked Myles and cooperated with him, the interview could mean anywhere from two to eight hundred dollars, depending on where Myles could sell the article. With a subject like Duncan Ely, who ranked with Artur Rubinstein and Vladimir Horowitz as one of the piano immortals, he'd have no trouble placing it. There was a good chance the *Times* Sunday magazine would buy it, which would make this early awakening well worthwhile.

Fifteen minutes later, Myles bounded up the stairs, shaved and dressed.

"How do I look?" he asked, taking the black coffee Paula handed him.

"Gorgeous. Do you have your tape recorder?"

"I thought I'd do this interview on clay tablets. A gim-mick."

"Ha ha. How about your TarGard?"

Both Myles and Paula smoked too much, and a year be-fore, they had begun using the black holders to cut down their tar intake. Unfortunately, they were always losing them.

"Believe it or not, it's in my pocket."

"Are you taking a cab to Sixty-third Street?"

"Yep. Money be damned. I'm off."

He set down his coffee mug, kissed Paula, then started down the stairs of their duplex.

"Buy some Clorets!" she called after him. "Your breath's horrible."

"I love you, too."

"Seriously."

"Okay. Clorets and a cherry Danish. I'll be kissing sweet. Bye."

She heard the door slam two floors below. Then she went downstairs to wash. Their only bathroom was small and connected their bedroom with Abby's. It had been di-lapidated when they moved in, but they had repaired the cracked tiles, painted the walls a cheery yellow, installed a new medicine chest, bought new shower curtains for the big old-fashioned clawfoot tub, and brightened the place with framed posters of early Shirley Temple movies. Paula had objected to the posters as too campy, but Myles was an old movie buff, and he said he liked to hum "The Good Ship Lollypop" while he shaved. Paula had given in.

After scrubbing her face with Yardley Lavender, she heard Abby getting dressed in her bedroom and wondered what she would do with her that day. Usually, Myles was home writing while Paula was at the small beachwear shop she and Maggie van Arsdale owned on Bleecker Street. Today, though, Myles would be out; and since the pre-Christmas season was their busiest time at the shop, Paula couldn't stay home. She decided to leave Abby at Maggie's, who had a full-time maid for her three kids. Maggie's husband, Chuck, was a doctor making a hand-some income after years of starving as an intern. Some-times Paula wished Myles had the security of a paying profession like medicine instead of a boom-or-bust profes-sion like writing. But, ultimately, she was glad he was what he was: a washed-out concert pianist turned writer, with one mystery novel selling tepidly on the paperback racks, two Channel 13 credits, a number of free-lance articles with which he earned his daily bread, and sixteen completed chapters of the Great American Novel.

After all, she thought, he's good, and that makes the difference. In the long run, we'll win bigger than Chuck and Maggie, and won't that be fun?

With that comforting thought, she put on her gray mini-dress, her matching gray stockings and her buckled shoes; touched her ears and throat with the perfume she was never without, Shalimar; then went in to kiss Abby.

Duncan Ely owned a five-floor brownstone on Sixty-third Street, between Madison and Park. As Myles got out of the cab, he glanced enviously at the handsome town houses that lined the block, their facades softened by the trees planted at the curb. One of the frustrations Myles found in interviewing celebrities was that their success always reminded him of his own insignificance. Wondering if his novels would ever bring him enough fame so that someday someone would interview *him,* he climbed the four steps to the front door and rang the bell. As he waited, he listened to the exciting dissonances of Prokofiev's Third Piano Sonata being played somewhere inside the house. Though the sound was muffled and distant, he recognized the brilliant technique and powerful bravura style as Duncan Ely's.

The door was opened by a cadaverous butler who admitted Myles to a long entrance hall with a black and white marble floor. At the end of the hall was a graceful staircase, its wall lined with a set of nineteenth-century etchings of the great composers, starting cheerfully with Vivaldi and ending gloomily with Papa Brahms.

"We'll have to wait till Mr. Ely's through playing," said the butler as he took Myles' coat. Myles nodded and stationed himself by the tall double doors leading into the living room of the house. After a few minutes, the sonata ended and the butler gingerly opened the doors. Myles followed him into an enormous room decorated in a starkly modern style that came as a surprise after the traditional entrance hall. The long sofa and sleek chairs were white, as were the walls and carpet, a device which dramatized the two enormous black Steinways, placed bow in bow at the end of the room, and the three gigantic op art paintings that dominated the other walls. In the corner by the pianos stood four thin, elongated Giacometti sculptures which stared lifelessly at Myles and the butler as they came in. A thin, elongated man rose from the left Steinway and also stared at them, though his look was anything but lifeless and struck Myles as being annoyed, if not actually hostile. It occurred to him this interview was going to be more difficult than he had supposed.

The butler announced him, then left him alone with the famous pianist. Since Duncan Ely was standing by the piano making no attempt to break the ice, Myles nervously set down his tape recorder and advanced toward him.

"It's very kind of you to see me this early, Mr. Ely," he said, wishing he could have thought of a more intelligent opener. As he came nearer, he saw that Ely's face, which must once have been handsome, was a mesh of wrinkles and that the staring eyes were festooned with huge bags. His thick, white hair was brushed and pomaded flat and hung long on the nape of his neck, in a rather dated Bohemian style. He must have been six feet two or three; and though he was past seventy, there wasn't an ounce of excess fat on his bony frame. Nor had age stooped him. He stood straight by the piano, watching Myles, giving an impression of supreme self-confidence and a sort of elegant arrogance that was reminiscent of the Ingres drawing of Paganini.

"I don't like to give interviews, Mr. Clarkson," he said, "so I hope we can make this brief."

"It can be as brief or as long as you want to make it, sir," said Myles rather testily. He extended his hand, thinking that if the hostile Mr. Ely didn't thaw, he'd back out of the interview. He knew from experience that if a subject refused to open up, it was a waste of time trying to write about him.

Ely frowned as he looked at Myles' outstretched hand. Then, to Myles' surprise, he reached out and took the hand, not to shake it but to inspect it. Silently, he looked at the long fingers. Then he pointed to Myles' left hand.

"May I?" he said.

Wondering if the old man might have mental problems, Myles held out his other hand. Ely took it eagerly and again looked at the fingers. Then he held the palm up and pressed his own hand against it.

"Stretch your fingers out, please," he said. Myles obeyed. "Both hands." Ely studied his fingers pressed against Myles'. Except for the age difference in the skin, the hands might have been identical.

"You have magnificent piano hands," said Ely, stepping back. "Have you ever played?"

Myles couldn't understand the older man's change of attitude. Suddenly he had become pleasant, if not ingratiating.

"I used to. In fact, I studied at the Juilliard and wanted to make a career of it. Unfortunately, the critics didn't share my enthusiasm."

"Critics! What do they know? You shouldn't have let that put you off. With hands like those—can you reach a twelfth?"

"Yes."

"I thought so. Great hands—great. Rachmaninoff hands." He gestured toward the keyboard. "I don't suppose you'd play me something?"

"Me?" Myles looked confused. "I'm out of practice—"

"That doesn't matter. Play anything. Some Chopin? You do the Études?"

"I *did* them, but it's been a long time—"

"Good! Here, sit down. Wait, let me find the score, or do you need one?"

"I'll need one."

"Here we go." He picked a score from the piles of music on the pianos and placed it on the rack. Then he came around behind Myles, who leafed uncertainly through the music then said, "I'll play the Fourth in C Sharp Minor, but I'm warning you there'll be mistakes."

"I know, I know. It doesn't matter. I'll really appreciate it. It's not often one finds a pair of hands like yours."

Myles tackled the étude, making a mistake in the second measure and starting over again.

"I told you it would be bad," he said.

"No, no, you're quite good. Excellent! Keep playing."

Myles obeyed, thinking that at least the old boy's change in attitude should make for a better interview. When he had finished the étude, playing it far below tempo and making numerous sloppy errors, he looked up to see a woman standing next to Duncan Ely. She looked about thirty, and her face, crowned with black hair, was hauntingly beautiful.

"Superb, Mr. Clarkson! Superb!" gushed the old man. "Roxanne, meet Mr. Clarkson. Mr. Clarkson, my daughter, Mrs. de Lancre. Look at his hands, my dear. Aren't they extraordinary?"

Roxanne smiled as she shook Myles' hand.

"You must forgive my father. Hands are sort of a hobby with him."

"Don't apologize for me!" snorted Duncan. "It's not every day you see hands like his, and it's something to get excited about. Well, now, you didn't come here to be fussed over. You're supposed to fuss over me, right? Coddle the old boy and humor him so he won't snap your head off, like he does most reporters?"

"That's the general idea," smiled Myles.

"Well, I'll turn on the charm and you'll see that all the stories they tell about Duncan Ely are untrue: he can be sweet as treacle. Roxanne, tell Bennet to bring us some coffee. I'll sit here on the sofa and Mr. Clarkson can sit in the chair with his tape recorder, and I'll blabber away for hours—only because of your hands, mind you! Otherwise, I'd have been surly as hell. We pianists must stick together. What's your first name?"

"Myles."

"Ah, yes, Myles. Myles was going to be a pianist, my dear, but he let the critics scare him off. Too bad. Ely's First Rule of Critics is: Treat them nice, and they'll kick you in the teeth. But ignore them like I've done for fifty years, and they'll fawn all over you. Do you live in New York, Myles, or out in that green Potemkin village they call Westchester?"

"My wife and I live downtown," said Myles, setting up his recorder. "We have the top two floors of an old house near Sheridan Square."

"Greenwich Village—good. A fine place to live, despite the hippies and tourists. All right, fire away with the questions. If you want to know when I first played the piano, it was when I was four. The first tune I banged out was 'Rule, Brittania,' and the first composer I fell in love with was Mozart. Now, seventy years later, I'm still in love with him, which is almost a record for a love affair, I'd say. But Mozart never palls: he's always fresh, witty, and charming. Do you know his two-piano Sonata in D?"

"I've played it."

"Good. Brush up the second piano part. We're having a

party here next Saturday night—bring your wife, and after dinner you and I will play the Mozart. Unless you've got other plans?"

"Well, no," said Myles, again surprised by the old man. "We'd be delighted. But—"

"But what?"

"Well, Mr. Ely, I'm really not very good anymore."

"Let me be the judge of that, young man. I say you're very good. I say with hands like that you should be playing the piano, not interviewing relics like me. So we'll play the Mozart, and maybe I can get you interested in music again. All right, what's your first question?"

Paula Clarkson and Maggie van Arsdale closed their Bleecker Street shop at six that evening and walked to Maggie's seventh floor co-op apartment overlooking Washington Square. Paula collected Abby, who had had a fine time watching a Jungle Boy movie on television with Maggie's kids; then they walked home. When they reached the red brick house the top two floors of which Paula and Myles had lucked into five years previously, it was quarter to seven and the two affable homosexuals who ran the antique shop on the ground floor were just closing. Paula waved to them as she searched for her key—their names, incredibly, were Random and House—then she unlocked her front door and followed Abby up the narrow stairs of their hundred-year-old house. The apartment was upside down in that the two bedrooms, bath, and tiny study were on the first floor, while the kitchen and living room were on the second. But this was no inconvenience; and the luxury of being the only resident tenants in a house in the middle of megalopolis made their rent-controlled paradise the envy of their friends.

Paula told Abby to take her bath while she cooked dinner. Then, kissing her pretty daughter, she went upstairs where she found Myles sitting in the small kitchen in the back of the house, drinking a glass of Almadén Chablis.

"How was the maestro?" she asked, kissing him.

"Very nice. Except he's got a thing about hands," replied Myles. As Paula put a chicken in the broiler, he told her of Duncan's strange behavior that morning. "It was lucky for me. I mean, he was hostile as hell when I came in. But after the hand business, he couldn't have been more cooperative. I got a damned good interview."

"But what's that mean, hands are his hobby? What does he do—collect them?"

Myles shrugged.

"How do I know?"

"And he wants you to play double piano with him next week?"

"Uh-huh. Don't ask me why, when he could get the best pros in the business to play with him. Anyway, it's sort of flattering. Do you want a sherry?"

"No, thanks. And, darling, not to be a nag, but don't drink the wine too fast."

Myles put on a mock-drunk face as he filled his glass.

"But I *like* to drink. I like to drink till I hear that little 'click' in my head—"

"Okay, Brick. What's his daughter like?"

"Mrs. de Lancre? Excluding present company, I'd say she's the most beautiful woman I've ever met."

Paula sat down at the small round table.

"I hope I don't have to start getting nervous?"

He laughed and reached across the table to take her hand.

"Not a chance. Roxanne's beautiful, but she sort of puts the chill in you. She watches over her father like a hawk —goes on all his concert tours and makes all the arrangements for him—I gather from what he told me she hardly has any life of her own at all."

"What about Mr. de Lancre?"

"Oh, she divorced him a long time ago. Ten years or more. At any rate, she seems happy with her father, but they're an odd pair. I still don't understand why he wants *me* to play Mozart with him. Me, whose debut had the distinction of receiving the most tepid reviews since Florence Foster Jenkins."

Though Myles could now refer to his Town Hall debut with casual flipness, Paula knew the memory still hurt him. Myles had had all the equipment for a successful musical career: extraordinary hands, great talent and a fine ear. What he had lacked was drive: the willingness to practice eight to ten hours a day. There was a streak of the daydreamer in Myles which was useful in his writing but which had been disastrous in his music, and which had resulted in an unprofessionally sloppy debut. She remembered his real despair at his failure. She remembered the seven months it took her to pull him out of the drunken

apathy he fell into and set him on a new career, filled with
new hope. She liked to think she was at least partially responsible for the discipline he had finally achieved in his
writing. Now, after six years, the hard work was beginning
to pay off, and he was on the verge of making it as a
writer. But Paula knew the piano was still his first love,
and whatever success he might achieve in literature, no
matter how welcome, would always be a second-best sub-
stitute for what might have been.

After dinner, he sat down at the ancient upright in the
living room and fumbled his way through the Mozart. His
technique was bad, the piano was flatted beyond endur-
ance, and the result was painfully amateur.

She couldn't help but agree that Duncan Ely had made
an unlikely choice for a piano partner.

"Thank God I haven't put on any weight since high
school," said Myles the following Saturday as he looked at
himself in the closet mirror. The dinner jacket was out of
style, but it still fit.

"It looks good on you," said Paula. "When was the last
time you wore it?"

"At Art Cohen's brother's Bar Mitzvah four years ago.
What are you wearing?"

"I can't make up my mind between the Balenciaga, the
Mainbocher, the Norell, or the Galanos—"

"Uh-huh. Greenwich Village's answer to Jackie Kennedy."

"So I'll wear the Ohrbach's."

She pulled out a lovely white evening gown with beaded
bodice that she'd splurged a hundred and twenty dollars
on the year before. Though Paula was able to buy most of
her clothes wholesale through her contacts on Seventh
Avenue, she still loved to shop and would periodically pay
a retail price to get something she'd fallen in love with.

"Try and look good," said Myles, adjusting his black tie.
"This should be a pretty fawncy crowd. We don't want to
look *too* much like poor cousins."

Paula said nothing, but his remark irritated her. During
the past week Myles had had two practice sessions with
Duncan Ely, and when he returned home his conversation
had become increasingly dominated by the pianist and his
daughter. Gone was his feeling that they were an "odd"
pair: now they could do no wrong. Roxanne was gor-

geous, Duncan's music was fantastic, their house was fabulous, they knew everybody who was anybody, they were kind, generous, witty, intelligent. . . . It had gotten on her nerves; and each time he had praised them, she had grown to like them less.

"Are you nervous about playing?" she asked, coolly.

"Panicked. But at least I don't have to play by memory. And Duncan promised to play loud if I start to screw up."

"Oh? It's 'Duncan' now?"

Myles grinned.

"Uh-huh. Buddy-buddy with the world's great, that's me. If the White House calls, tell them I'm in the john."

He went into the bathroom, closing the door behind him as he always did, even when he was only brushing his teeth.

Paula completed her makeup, brushed her hair, and dabbed on her Shalimar. Myles didn't have to tell her to look good. She had already made up her mind to look her best when she met Mr. Ely and his daughter. She wasn't about to let the "gorgeous" Roxanne think Paula Clarkson was a frump.

It was snowing heavily when they got out of the cab in front of Duncan's town house, and Paula hung on her husband's arm as they climbed the steps to the front door. Myles rang the bell, then gestured upward at the handsome facade of the house.

"Nice?"

"Very nice. Does he own it?"

"Yep."

"It must be worth a fortune."

"*He's* worth a fortune. Beside the quarter million that rolls in each year from record royalties and personal appearances, he's stashed away almost four million in blue chips and tax-free municipals. Of course, some of that he inherited from his wife, but it shows piano playing *can* pay."

"When did his wife die?"

"About twenty years ago. Wait till you see Bennet, the butler. He's so stuffy he makes Arthur Treacher look *sportivo*."

The door was opened by Bennet (How wonderful some people still have butlers! thought Paula, who had more than a passing interest in the "good life" she hoped Myles'

career would some day enable them to lead) and they
were ushered into the long entrance foyer. After giving
Bennet their coats and removing their boots, they went
into the living room, where a dozen elegant men and
women were standing around in groups of twos or threes,
looking almost as posed as the Giacometti statues.

Paula drank in the scene. Then Roxanne came up to
them, smiling and extending her hand.

"You must be Paula," she said in her warm, low voice.
"I'm Roxanne de Lancre. I'm so delighted you could
come."

Roxanne was wearing a black satin gown in the style of
the early thirties which showed off her spectacular figure
to advantage. The white skin of her bare shoulders, arms
and breast seemed almost chalky against the ebony satin
and the bloody redness of the ruby bracelet that dangled
on her wrist. She gave the impression of a maturity
greater than her age, an effortless charm and a subdued
sensuality. Though her thin lips were smiling warmly, her
violet eyes were cold, and Paula thought that Myles' remark was justified—Roxanne did put the chill in you.

She led them around the room, introducing them to the
other guests. The British ambassador to the U.N. was there,
with his wife. So were the chairman of the board of one
of the biggest banks in the country; one of the vice presi-
dents of RCA Victor Records, for whom Duncan recorded
exclusively; the current hottest musical director on Broad-
way; Philip Rosen, Duncan's manager, an affable, bald
pipe-smoker; Dame Agatha Renfrew, the English pianist;
Princess Ina Andrassy, a Scottish beauty who had earned
houses in Acapulco, Sardinia, and Paris from her first two
husbands; and finally, Duncan himself.

Paula was surprised at the enthusiastic friendliness with
which he greeted her. He clasped her hand and said, "And
here's the woman I woke up on the phone last Saturday."

Paula smiled.

"How did you know that? I thought I sounded bright as
a penny."

"I won't tell you how I know when I've wakened a
woman, but take my word for it: I know. You're as pretty
as Myles said you were. Roxanne, you take care of Myles.
I want to talk to his lovely wife. What would you like to
drink?"

"A sherry, please. Manzanilla, if you have it."

"I'm afraid we're not very big sherry drinkers in this house. All we have is oloroso."

Paula didn't like sweet sherry, particularly before dinner, but she accepted the drink. As Roxanne and Myles joined Princess Andrassy and Philip Rosen, Duncan led Paula to a white chair. He sat down beside her and leaned close. He had the knack of concentrating his entire attention on a person—or at least giving the appearance of it. Paula noticed his eyes were violet, like his daughter's. Oddly, they were also cold.

"I can't tell you how much I've enjoyed meeting your husband. I rarely give interviews, but for once I'm glad I did. I like him immensely. He's a fine young man, and a tremendous musical talent. There's nothing more exciting for us old war-horses than to find talent in the young."

Paula wondered why he thought Myles' talent so extraordinary when a number of critics had found it to be so painfully ordinary.

"That's kind of you to say, Mr. Ely. But I like to think Myles' writing talent is his greatest gift."

"Perhaps. I've never read anything of his, though I'm sure it's excellent. But you'll forgive me for being biased in favor of music. Now tell me all about yourself. Everything. I'm an incredibly nosy man, and I like to find out all I can about people. You're not a native New Yorker—I can tell from your accent. Massachusetts?"

"Close. Connecticut."

"Hartford?"

"Right, Professor Higgins."

Duncan Ely was more than nosy. He was a grand inquisitor. All through dinner, which was magnificent, he pried information out of Paula with a humor and tact that prevented her from showing her annoyance—though annoyed she was. She told him everything: about her parents, now both dead; her childhood; her schooling; her meeting with Myles, their marriage, Abby, her shop, her friends, her likes and dislikes, her politics, her religion, even whether she and Myles were planning another child, which they weren't. By the time they got up and moved back to the living room for brandy and coffee, Paula couldn't resist remarking, "I feel rather defensive."

"Why?"

"You know everything about me, and I know nothing about you."

He smiled.

"That's a trick one learns as one grows older. Besides, you can read your husband's article and learn everything you want to about me. The statistics, that is. If you really want to know me, listen to me play. My music is me, and I'm my music. I'm really a very uncomplicated person. Brandy?"

Paula thought, on the contrary, he was a very complicated person who tried to give the appearance of being simple. She had the odd feeling he had a definite purpose in quizzing her, and the reason, whatever it was, was more devious than a mere interest in a dinner partner. Devious? Yes, devious. She decided Duncan Ely was a devious man.

Myles had been seated next to Roxanne during dinner. Now he rejoined his wife on the long sofa.

"What did you think of that meal?" he whispered. She could smell the wine on his breath and hoped it wouldn't affect his playing.

"Julia Child would have swooned with ecstasy."

"And that Romanée-Conti! You know how much that stuff costs?"

"I know you'd better get some coffee in you, or you're going to flub the musicale. What were you and Roxanne so chummy about?"

"Oh, she was asking me a lot of questions about myself. You know."

"I know. Big Daddy put me through the grinder too. Do you think they're spies or something?"

"Definitely. Narcotics agents, trying to find out how we're smuggling in all that hashish. Sshhh—Maestro's going to play."

It was a custom, whenever Duncan entertained in his home, for him to play after dinner. After the brandy and coffee were passed, he went to the left Steinway and sat down. The guests watched him with the anticipation of true music lovers being offered a feast.

"Usually, we start with Bach and work up to Stravinsky," he said. "But tonight, I'm reversing the order. Not that I'm playing anything modern: that's too hard to take on a full stomach." Laughter. "But I'll start with something lush and work backwards to Mozart, at which time young Mr. Clarkson will join me for the two-piano Sonata in D. To begin, however, a little Liszt-Busoni. The 'Mephisto Waltz.'"

A murmur of excitement from the guests, for this was one of Duncan's famous bravura pieces. Then silence. Paula found herself fascinated by the effortless way the aging man controlled his audiences, no matter how large or small. He seemed to have that uncanny communication with them, that ability to manipulate them, that separated stars from mere performers. He stared at the keyboard, as if studying it like a surgeon preparing to cut into a patient. Then, at precisely the right moment, he leaned forward and attacked the D sharp grace note. From the piano pulsed the nervous waltzing E's with their biting D sharps on the downbeat, soft and mysterious like some eldritch orchestra tuning up on "Bald Mountain." Then a B was added, the open fifths sounding sepulchrally hollow. An F sharp and then a C sharp were piled on top of the E minor fifth, the biting waltz building to a maniacal dissonant shriek. Then three soft chords; silence; four whispering figures; and the waltz theme started again. The melodramatic nineteenth-century music, which could sound so hackneyed in the hands of a lesser artist, took on a surprising freshness and vitality when played by Duncan. As the music swirled, smoked, shrieked and thundered, Paula found herself transfixed. Duncan knew how to coax every effect out of the piano. His sensuous legato in the dolce amoroso passage; his pyrotechnical brilliance in the vivace fantastico section; his hammering power in the brutalmente octaves seemed to conjure Mephistopheles himself out of the strings and hammers, and she thought she could actually see the shrieking witches at the sabbath, twirling in a Satanic ecstasy until they exploded in a final burst of perverted demonic lust. As the number howled to a double forte close, the listeners sat stunned—the ultimate accolade. Then they burst into applause.

"Christ," whispered Myles, "it's like listening to Liszt himself!"

He looked completely awed, like a little boy.

Duncan, the master showman, stood up, wiped his sweat-drenched forehead, grinned at the applause and held up his hands for silence.

"If you play Liszt, you don't need to do calisthenics." Laughter. "And now, something less vivid: the Schubert A Major."

He sat down again and launched into the pellucid sonata with a tenderness one wouldn't have thought possible so soon after the Satanic fireworks. Paula's eyes wandered slowly around the beautiful room filled with such beautiful people and such beautiful music. What a rich life he leads! she thought. She could understand now why Myles had been so impressed with Duncan Ely. The man might be strange or even devious, but there was no denying he led an extraordinarily glamorous existence.

Her eyes rested on Roxanne, who was sitting by herself in back of the others. The gorgeous black satin body was relaxed; the cold, violet eyes were riveted on her father. Except they didn't seem cold anymore. They seemed hot.

A large black Labrador had curled itself at her feet. It was a beautiful animal—huge, powerful and sleek, its coat almost as satiny as Roxanne's gown.

It was looking directly at Paula.

For some reason, she suddenly felt cold.

Myles played badly.

He was nervous, and had had too much wine. While he didn't make any jarring mistakes, his technique and tone were poor. Compared to Duncan's masterful rendition of the Mozart, Myles seemed like a novice. But when they had finished, Duncan raved about his performance.

"Magnificent! Look at those hands! Just look at them! Rachmaninoff reincarnated!"

The Rachmaninoff hands were at that moment inserting a cigarette in a TarGard and lighting it nervously.

"You smoke too much," chided Duncan. "A man with your talent should take care of his body. Cigarettes can kill you—don't believe this 'harmful' business they put on the packs: they can *kill* you. You ought to grind that thing out and never smoke another. I've never smoked, thank God."

This was hardly calculated to improve Myles' sense of well-being. Coughing, he added brandy to his list of vices.

Three brandies later, he was looking bleary, and Paula decided it was time to leave. Duncan had cornered her again on the sofa, asking her more questions about herself. Now she stood up and extended her hand.

"Mr. Ely, I've really enjoyed myself enormously."

"You're not going?"

"I'm afraid we have to. I promised my sitter we'd be

home by midnight, and I don't dare be late for my sitter. But it was so pleasant meeting you and your daughter, and I loved the music. Thank you so much."

Duncan was on his feet, his arm around her waist, leading her to the door.

"I was delighted you could come, my dear. Delighted. And your husband!" Myles had joined them, and Duncan took his arm. "A fine pianist, and a fine person. Have you finished your article yet, Myles?"

Myles nodded sleepily. Paula knew he was about one drink away from a stupor.

"I'm typing it tomorrow."

"I'd like to read it before you submit it to a magazine."

"Oh, sure, that goes without saying. We'll send it to the *Times* first. They should snap it up."

He belched. Paula winced.

They were in the front hall now, putting on boots and coats. Roxanne came out, followed by the black Labrador. Smiling her beautiful smile, she shook Paula's hand.

"I was so glad to have met you," she said, "though I'm afraid I didn't get a chance to talk to you."

"I monopolized her," chuckled Duncan. "By the way, did you meet Robin? Come here, Robin." He squatted down and reached out to the huge dog, who came over, his tail wagging happily, and licked his master's hands. "Isn't he a beauty? Robin, this is Mrs. Clarkson."

As Paula leaned over to pat the dog's head, he looked up at her and growled. She quickly drew back.

"Robin's bark's worse than his bite," said Duncan. "He always growls till he gets to know you."

Paula forced a smile but thought she would prefer not "getting to know" Robin if she could help it.

In the taxi racing down Park Avenue through the thick snow that had already dumped two inches on the city, Myles sank back into the seat and mumbled sleepily, "Well? What did you think of them?"

"They're very nice," replied Paula.

But she was lying. Despite their friendliness, their charm and their hospitality, she didn't like them. She didn't like them at all.

*

By the time Myles had paid the sitter, he was beginning to sober up. He took a Bromo-Seltzer, then undressed and got in bed beside Paula. For a while he stared at the ceiling, smoking a cigarette. Paula lighted one for herself with a matchbook she had taken from Duncan's dining room. It was black, with the initials *D.M.E.* printed in red on the cover.

"What are you thinking about?" she asked, putting the matchbook on the bed table.

"Why some people make it and others don't."

"You'll make it," she whispered. She leaned over and put her head on his smooth, bare chest, running her hand softly over his fine skin. "You'll have everything he has some day."

He didn't say anything. Then he ground out the cigarette and began making love. He was gentle and unaggressive, as always. But Paula loved it, as she loved him. Though she didn't consider herself a highly sexed woman, there was nothing that soothed her more or that she enjoyed more intensely than her husband's lovemaking—running her hands over his strong, handsome face, feeling the warmth of his muscled body. For a second, she wondered if Roxanne might feel the same way about him. She had certainly displayed a more than polite interest in Myles that night. Then she dismissed the thought. Though there didn't seem to be any potential lovers at the party, she was sure Roxanne's love life was amply provided for. Sensuous, beautiful creatures like that never had to go begging. Besides, Myles had always been faithful, and he wasn't the type who played around. She decided she had nothing to worry about.

She hoped.

"Myles," she whispered, after they had finished. He had turned on his right side, as he always did before going to sleep.

"What?"

"I ruv you."

"Mmm. I ruv you, too, Cio Cio."

A minute later, he was snoring peacefully.

Maggie van Arsdale had been Paula's roommate at Middlebury. Later, when they had renewed their friendship in New York, Maggie had asked Paula if she'd like to go into business with her. The idea had begun as idle chatter; it ended by both of them putting up three thousand dollars (Paula's share coming from her father's small estate), renting a store on Bleecker west of Seventh Avenue, and operating a shop called the Beach Bum. They carried the standard beachware, plus kookier items Maggie designed herself. And though Bleecker Street was a long way from the beach, the first year they broke even and the second year they netted two thousand dollars profit each. Maggie was bright, imaginative and much more aggressive than Paula. She had streaked blond hair and a go-go personality, and she was already talking about opening another store uptown.

"Not till we're clearing five thousand a year each," said Paula, who was not as eager as Maggie to take on the added risk and responsibility of another store.

"Then we'd better start looking, O cautious one, because we're going to clear that *this* year," said Maggie. And the way the pre-Christmas business had been booming, it looked as if she might be right.

However, the Monday after Duncan's party, business was slow. And by five thirty, they were ready to close.

"Where the hell *is* everybody?" fumed Maggie, looking out the gaily Christmased window at the near-empty street.

"Monday's always dead," said Paula.

"Not two weeks before Christmas, and not when it's forty-two out and clear."

"All that melting snow is keeping people at home. Who wants to wade through dirty slush?"

Five minutes later, Duncan Ely walked in. He was immensely charming and told Paula he had been in the Village and decided to take a look at her shop. Maggie, badly concealing her excitement at having such a celebrity on the premises, showed him their line. To her delight, he bought a hundred and fifty dollars' worth of presents, including a sixty-dollar beach robe for Roxanne.

"I always make a fool of myself at Christmas," he said, writing a check as Paula and Maggie gift-wrapped his purchases. "Even though I should hate it."

"Hate it? Why?"

"Because my birthday's December twenty-four. Can you imagine a worse time to be born? I get cheated out of all my birthday presents. Let's see: you and Myles live near here, don't you?"

"Three blocks."

"Well, then, why don't you let me take you out to dinner? There's a marvelous Armenian restaurant down here —do you like Armenian cooking?"

Paula hesitated.

"That's very kind of you, Mr. Ely—"

"Duncan."

"Duncan, but we really can't—"

"Can't? Why not? Ah, I know: no baby-sitter. That's easily solved. We'll bring your daughter too. I'd like to meet her."

Paula didn't like his "dropping by" the store, and she didn't like the idea of being obligated to him for another meal. So she invited him to dinner instead. To her annoyance, he accepted enthusiastically.

"And *I'll* do the cooking," he added.

"Don't be silly—"

"But I'd like to. Food's one of my hobbies. No, since you weren't expecting me, let me do the whole dinner. I insist. Mrs. van Arsdale, my car's outside: can we drop you home?"

Maggie readily accepted. They closed the shop, and Bennet carried the packages out to the gleaming black Rolls-Royce.

"What a beautiful car!" said Maggie as she climbed in the back seat.

"Yes, the English may be in trouble as a country, but they still can't be beat on cars, Scotch and tweeds. Music, too. Some of the most exciting young composers are English. Bennet, Mrs. van Arsdale lives at 35 Washington Square West. Then we'll come back to Bleecker Street to do our shopping. There's no better place in New York to buy food than the Village, unless it's the Ninth Avenue Markets. That's because the Italians down here insist on the best, and they get it."

Though Paula cringed at the thought of Duncan's reaction to her antediluvian kitchen, he seemed completely unfazed by the cramped quarters and antique oven and refrigerator. He set down his bulging grocery sacks, then shooed her out. "Give me twenty minutes for the preliminaries. Then I'll come out and have a drink and you can show me your apartment."

"Are you sure I can't help?"

"Absolutely. I like to practice alone, and I like to cook alone. Now, out! And relax. This is your evening to do nothing."

He closed the kitchen door, and Paula went into the living room, trying to convince herself she shouldn't feel so annoyed at his imposing himself on her evening. Twenty minutes later he emerged, his sleeves rolled up and a smile on his wrinkled face.

"You'll start smelling something very good in a minute or two. You could use some more counter space in that kitchen."

"I certainly could," agreed Paula, embarrassed that the kitchen had, after all, bothered him.

"But this living room is delightful—really delightful. And a skylight! Was it a studio once?"

He looked around at the large, airy room on which Myles and Paula had lavished so much time, love and spare cash. She hoped he would comment on the French desk she had found on Second Avenue, or the white linen curtains she had hemmed herself, or the bookcases she and Myles had slaved to build. At least she hoped for some remark on the surrealist paintings by the Korean artist in whom she and Myles had invested, hoping his prices would eventually soar—which they hadn't. Instead, all he

mentioned was the skylight, which was dirty. She was
fiercely proud of the once rundown apartment they had
turned into a charmingly elegant home, and she felt hurt
by Duncan's condescending disinterest which he had
masked with the feeble word "delightful."

"We think it was a studio," said Myles, making Duncan
a Scotch.

"I lived in the Village back in the Maxwell Bodenheim
days. I loved it then and still do. It's one of the best places
in the city to live, though I understand it's getting expensive—but then, isn't everything?"

Abby, looking pretty in a red dress, was watching the
celebrated pianist with interest. Though she was usually
shy with strangers, she mustered her courage and said, "I
saw you on television once, Mr. Ely."

"You did? When?" His tone and smile were avuncular.

"A couple of months ago. You were playing with some
symphony. Do you know Leonard Bernstein?"

"I do indeed."

"I think he's wonderful, don't you?"

"I'm a great admirer of Lennie's. Do you like music?"

"Oh, yes. I like the Beatles a lot."

What's he after? thought Paula as Duncan rattled on,
ingratiating himself with Abby, asking her all sorts of questions about her school and her friends—just as he had
done to her parents—all with a charm Paula couldn't help
but feel was forced. *It's almost as if he's studying us,* she
thought. Yes, that's exactly what he's doing: he's studying
us.

But why?

The dinner was filets of sole with an unusual curry
sauce, rice, some delicious fresh peas from Mexico, an en-
dive and raisin salad, and for dessert a rich creamy French
custard topped with plump strawberries. To accompany
this feast, Duncan had bought three bottles of Hermitage
Blanc '62. Paula had no idea how he had prepared the
meal with such apparent ease, but she had to admit the
sole was the best she'd ever eaten. Even Myles, who was a
steak-and-potatoes man who usually shunned more elabo-
rate cuisine, even he was impressed.

Throughout dinner, Duncan continued to question
them.

"Tell me about your novel," he said to Myles as he re-filled the wine glasses. "Does it have a good story? That's what I like: adventure, plot and suspense. I'm not very big on the so-called 'intellectual' novel."

"Well, it certainly has a complicated story," said Myles. "In fact, it's so complicated that I'm a little lost myself."

"What's it about?"

"It's the history of an American family through three generations, beginning at the turn of the century and coming down to the present."

"Sounds like *The Forsyte Saga.*"

"It is, in a way. It's the kind of novel that's not very fashionable anymore, but I like it. Of course, I'm putting in a lot of sex to help it sell."

"Ah, the more sex the better! That's why I like Ian Fleming's books: action, suspense and *sex*. I met Fleming once. Quite an interesting fellow. What's the name of your book?"

"The working title is *The Dark Side of the Moon,* but I'm going to think up a better one."

"What's wrong with that? I think it's good. Sort of—what's the word critics are always using?—'evocative.'"

"It's also sort of meaningless."

Duncan wiped his mouth.

"If you're looking for a publisher, Sydney Raymont's one of my best friends. I'd be glad to put in a good word for you."

"I already have a publisher."

"But Sydney Raymont's not just *a* publisher: he's *the* publisher. If he takes you on, he can give your book the finest advertising and presentation. He can make you."

Myles looked at Paula. She knew what he was thinking. Sydney Raymont was bait any writer would rise to. She turned to Duncan.

"The problem is, Myles has promised this novel to the people who published his mystery last year."

"Did they give him an advance on royalties?"

"No. . . ."

"Then he doesn't have any obligation to them, does he?"

"Well, I think he does."

"Nonsense, my dear. In anything creative—and I consider performing almost as creative as writing—your first obligation has to be to yourself. If Myles has a chance to meet the top publisher in the country, he shouldn't pass it up. But of course, it's up to you. I think we have one more bottle of wine in the kitchen. Shall we finish it off with the salad?"

As he went into the kitchen, Paula stared sullenly at the candles on the table. She disliked Duncan's involving himself in her husband's writing career, though she could do nothing but thank him for his friendly offer. She disliked even more his cynical attitude, though she had to admit there was a lot of truth in what he said. She wished, with a degree of intensity that surprised her, that he would leave the house and never see them again.

He brought the last bottle of wine from the kitchen and filled the glasses.

Over coffee, Duncan brought up Sydney Raymont again.

"Every year I have a New Year's Eve party at the house. I can't stand going out on New Year's—too many drunks—so I ask people in. Anyway, Sydney and his wife will be there, so why don't you two plan to come? It can't do you any harm to meet him, at least."

Myles glanced at Paula, who frowned a no. Then he looked back at Duncan.

"We'd be delighted to come."

"Good. Do you know Bach's 'Italian Concerto'?"

"I used to."

"Look over the score. We'll play that to impress Sydney. He loves Bach."

"But—" Paula blurted out the word, then stopped. Duncan turned and smiled at her. The two candles, having burned down, gave his face an eerie appearance as they lighted its wrinkles from below.

"What's the matter, my dear? Did you have other plans for New Year's?"

"No, it's just—" She wanted to say, *Let us alone!* Instead, she said, "It's just that I'm not sure about a baby-sitter. They're so hard to get on New Year's Eve."

Duncan laughed.

"Baby-sitters again! Sometimes I think the world's being taken over by them."

"Taken?" said Myles. "They've already took. But we've got some time, and I know we can get one of the N.Y.U. students if Mrs. Angelloti can't come."

"Good. Then it's settled. Lots of champagne, lots of caviar and lots of music. I guarantee a good time. That was a damned fine dinner if I do say so myself—which I do. I don't believe in being modest, as you've probably noticed. If you're good, toot your own horn, I always say. Because no one's going to toot it for you—right?"

After Duncan had gone, Myles turned on Paula.

"What the hell got into you tonight?"

She was washing the dishes in their undersized sink.

"I didn't think anything 'got into me.' "

"Get off it. You hardly said two words the whole evening. And you couldn't have made it more obvious you didn't want to go to his place New Year's Eve if you'd written it on the wall in blood. What's the matter?"

Paula carefully stacked the Wedgwood dinner plates that had belonged to her grandmother.

"It's just that I don't know what he's after, and it bothers me."

"Who says he's after anything?"

"I do. I don't believe a man as successful as Duncan Ely is suddenly going to start gushing over two people like us. It doesn't make sense!"

"Did it ever occur to you he might like us?"

"Why should he? We're half his age—less! We're nobodies. Why is he going to start asking us into his charmed little circle of celebrities and fawning over us? You heard him: he said you have to be selfish—"

"He said 'obligated to yourself first.' Quote accurately."

"That means selfish. *He's* selfish, though he's trying to act like he isn't. So what's he have to gain by being so nice to us? And I don't believe he's doing it just because he thinks we're witty or charming or talented or something, because we're not *that* witty or charming by a long shot. And why's he studying us? Because that's exactly what he's doing, asking six million questions, practically snooping through the bureau drawers. Why?"

"Because he knows we have the key to the Pentagon's secret code."

"Be serious!"

"*You* be serious. The man likes us—it's that simple! Why make such a big tsimmus out of it?"

Paula came over and put her arms around his neck.

"Hey, your hands are all wet—"

"I know. But kiss me anyway."

He kissed her. She eased onto his lap.

"I'm sorry. Maybe I am making a tsimmus out of it. But it's just that he . . . gives me the creeps, I guess."

"The last thing I'd call Duncan Ely is creepy."

"Well, he is to me."

He kissed her neck.

"All right, he's creepy. He's Dracula. He wants our blood."

"With all his talk about liking sexy novels, maybe he wants our bodies. Mine—or yours."

Myles let out a low whistle.

"He really *does* bug you, doesn't he?"

"At least it would make it more understandable, wouldn't it?"

"He may be after you, but me? Huh-uh. Duncan used to have the reputation of being one of the swingingest old letches going. He may have shot his wad now, but he still likes girls."

"All right, what about Roxanne? I bet she'd like to get her coils around you."

"Sounds great."

"Myles!"

"Get off it. You know I'm no letch. Besides, if Roxanne wants a lover, she's not going to have to go very far to find one. She's just the slightest bit good-looking, you know."

"I know. Why do you think I'm so nervous?"

"Well, don't be. They're just two people who are being friendly—period. It does happen, you know—even in New York."

Paula got up from his lap and went back to the sink.

"Well, I still wish they'd let us alone. If nothing else, he's taking you away from the novel with all this practicing you're doing during the day."

"I'm not doing that much practicing."

"Myles, it's Paulie, remember? Paulie who knows all, sees all? Paulie who comes home and finds ashtray on piano filled with cigarette butts, and ashtray next to typewriter downstairs clean as proverbial whistle? Now, we played games last week. But let's not play games this week, okay? The novel's the important thing, not how you play double piano with Duncan Ely."

Myles looked grumpy, as he always did when the question of his self-discipline was brought up.

"But if he introduces me to Sydney Raymont, isn't that important too?"

"Not if you don't have any novel finished to show him. Mr. Raymont's not going to publish sixteen chapters."

For a while neither of them spoke as Paula continued to wash dishes and Myles sulked. She didn't like to dig at him about his writing, but she felt in this case she was justified. After a few minutes, Myles shrugged off his grumpiness. Hé came over to the sink and put his arms around her.

"Don't worry. The old muse is churning away. I'll do three more chapters this week."

"Promise?"

"Scout's honor. Truce about Duncan Ely, boy letch?"

She put the last plate in the drain.

"Okay. Truce about Duncan Ely."

"Hey, Paulie—look! There's a dove in your kitchen! A real dove!"

She looked at the empty counter where he was pointing, then turned around, laughing.

"You crazy nut, how can I stay mad at you?"

"Watch those wet hands—"

"Kiss me, you fool! Sweep me away from the drudgery of my household chores to your desert tent and make mad love to me!"

"Would you believe the bedroom?"

She kissed him, relaxing at the touch of his mouth against hers.

"I'll be down as soon as I rinse," she purred.

"Forget the Goddamn dishes."

"Talked me into it." She ran her hand through his thick black hair. "Myles, I ruv you."

"Yeah, I ruv you, Cio Cio. But not if you get dishwater in my hair."

Leaving the dishes in the sink, she followed him downstairs to the bedroom.

3

The stores outdid themselves in putting on their Christmas finery. Saks put up a huge dazzling tree instead of its usual pipe organ; across the street, Rockefeller Center was a gay baroque pageant with the mammoth fir towering above it. Paula took Abby shopping with her one night to let her see the city sparkling. Then one morning, she took off from the Beach Bum to buy the important presents in secret. She had carefully saved two hundred dollars for Christmas, and she had insisted to Myles he spend no more than a hundred. Now she bought him a pair of gold cuff links at Cartier and three shirts at Brooks. Then she went to F. A. O. Schwartz and bought a fabulous toy poodle for Abby that barked, walked and wagged its tail. The fifty dollars she had left she spent on books, toys and a pretty brown coat for her daughter. Then, bankrupt but happy, she went back to the Beach Bum to try and make some more money.

She said nothing more to Myles about Duncan Ely. She decided perhaps she had been unfair to the man who, after all, could be accused of nothing worse than nosiness. And the more she thought about meeting Sydney Raymont, the more she liked the idea. Paula knew the value of contacts in the publishing world.

However, she knew Myles was still goofing off. He was clever enough to dump the cigarette butts into the typewriter ashtray, but he didn't fool her. Still, it was Christmas. He had worked so long on the novel—perhaps it was better for him to get away from it awhile. She was wise

36

enough to know no one could force a writer to work except the writer himself.

She read Myles' article, which his agent had submitted
to the *Times*. It was well written and interesting, like talking to Duncan for a half hour. Interspersed in the dia-
logue were the biographical facts: his birth in London in
1893; his studying with Mandyczewski; his career as a
prodigy; his brilliant debut just before the World War; his
work for British Intelligence during the war; his trium-
phant return to his career after the Armistice; his first
marriage to a Frenchwoman which ended in divorce, and
his second marriage to an American which resulted in his
moving to New York in the twenties and becoming completely Americanized; the death of his second wife and his
emergence as the grand old man of the piano.

But even though the article was interesting, Paula felt
something had been left out, something she couldn't define
but which she nevertheless sensed. It was the public Duncan Ely in the article; the Duncan Ely he liked to show.
The real Duncan Ely wasn't there.

But Paula wasn't sure what the real Duncan Ely was.

On the morning of the twenty-first, she and Myles taxied to Kennedy to meet Myles' mother. Janet Clarkson,
who lived in Fort Lauderdale, was a dynamic Lady Clairol
blonde who had buried three husbands and now sold
houses while she kept an eye out for number four. Every
year she came to New York to spend Christmas with her
son. And every year she stumbled off the plane looking
like a suntanned zombie, thanks to the tranquilizers she
stuffed herself with to combat her morbid fear of flying.

"Thank God you came to get me," she gasped as Myles
took her arm. "One more Librium and I'd be out cold."

"How was the flight?"

"Awful. We bumped all the way. Besides, there was a
sinister little man that I was sure was going to hijack the
plane and take us all to Cuba. If I have any sense, I'll go
back on a bus. Whoever heard of hijacking a bus?"

That night she came down to the apartment for dinner
and to help trim the Scotch pine Myles had bought. Abby
adored her grandmother and could barely be restrained
from tearing off the red and green wrappings of the big
Christmas presents this fairy godmother from Fort Lauderdale had brought her. To calm her, she was put to
work placing Swedish wooden angels and glass balls on the

boughs. The trimming took three hours. When it was finished, Paula plugged in the strands of tiny white bulbs. As the tree blinked to life, Abby oohed her rhapsodic approval. Then Paula said, "All right, young lady. You know what time it is?"

Abby moaned but stoically accepted her fate as her mother took her down to bed. When Paula came back up she said to Janet, "You're certainly making her Christmas with those packages. All she could talk about was 'Grandma.'"

"She makes *my* Christmas," said Janet, sipping a Scotch. "By the way, she told me she'd love to get a dog. I thought I'd better check with you two first before I went to look for one."

Myles held up his hand.

"Dogs are out—period. There's not room in this place for a dog. And the last thing I want is to have to walk some mutt around the block every ten minutes."

"All right, no dogs. Are you having Abby's friends in on Christmas Day like last year?"

"Yes, with their parents," said Paula.

"I think that's a marvelous idea. She had such a good time. Who's D.M.E.?"

She had picked up the black matchbook Paula had taken from Duncan's town house and was lighting a cigarette.

"Oh, it must be Duncan Ely," said Paula.

Janet looked interested. "Where did you meet him?"

Myles explained.

"Well, since you've interviewed him you must know all about the murder!" said Janet.

Paula looked surprised.

"What murder?"

"*The* murder! The murder of his wife, of course. It happened in forty-eight or forty-nine, I can't remember which."

"You didn't say anything about his wife being murdered in the article," said Paula to Myles. "You just said she'd died."

Myles shrugged.

"Duncan asked me not to mention it. He's very sensitive about it, naturally. Besides, it wasn't a murder. They proved that. It was an accident."

"Accident, my eye!" snapped Janet. "I remember reading about it in the papers, and everybody said it was a murder then. Except they tried to hush it up afterwards."

"Was it his second wife?"

"Yes. She was an heiress, very glamorous—"

"Roxanne's mother?"

"Yes," said Myles.

"Anyway, they were at Saint Moritz or Zermatt or somewhere—"

"Saint Moritz."

"Yes, on a skiing holiday. And she and Ely went up on the slopes one morning, except she never came down. They sent out searching parties, and that afternoon they found her up on the mountain. She'd had her throat torn out."

"Torn *out?*"

"That's right. By a wolf or a dog or something."

"Good Lord! But why did they think it was murder?"

"Because there were not only a lot of paw prints around her body, there were also *foot*prints. Some man's."

"Did they ever find him?"

"No."

"But mightn't it have been someone who came up after the animal had attacked her? You know, and then ran off to get the police or whatever?"

Janet finished her Scotch.

"It might have been, except it wasn't."

"Mother," interrupted Myles testily, "you know the police discounted that whole story about the mysterious footprints. They said it was a dog, period. That was the end of it."

"It might have been the end of it for them, but if you ask me they dismissed it because they couldn't explain it."

"Explain what?" insisted Paula.

Janet looked at her.

"Explain the fact that while there were a lot of footprints around the body, there were none coming to it and none going away from it. There were only paw prints going away."

"You mean, the man was just *there?* He appeared out of thin air and then vanished?"

"That's right. And it was fresh powder snow."

Myles snickered.

"Uh-huh. It was a werewolf. Lon Chaney, Jr. Or Batman. He *flew* away. What you forgot to mention, Mother, is that it was not only fresh powder snow, there was also a strong wind—"

"Oh, baloney. Then why weren't *all* the prints covered up? Why weren't the paw prints covered? No, that wind theory's no good. And don't tell me the man skied away, because he would have left ski tracks—"

"Which they found!"

"Yes, *after* the police and the reporters had mucked up the snow. They didn't notice them when they first got there, though."

"And the police decided that whoever the man was, he had found the body by accident, gotten scared and skied away, which is perfectly reasonable. Plus there was a rabid dog in Saint Moritz whom they found the next day who had blood on his muzzle and whom they shot. End of 'mysterious disappearing footprints' and end of 'murder.' And can you blame Duncan for trying to keep the story hushed up, with ghouls like you around?"

His mother shrugged.

"Maybe I'm a ghoul. But if you ask me, nobody ever really explained it satisfactorily. And it was a very nice windfall for Mr. Ely, who inherited the wife's estate—a couple of million, as I recall."

Myles groaned.

"Talk about innuendo! Yes, Mother, this is the way it was done: Duncan told me himself. He had specially built paw-print shoes which he slipped on, sneaked up to his wife, bit her throat out, took off the paw-print shoes and made a lot of footprints, then put them back on, skipped off and inherited her millions. Except for one minor flaw: he was never out of sight of at least six other people the entire day."

Janet stood up.

"All right, it wasn't him. I don't know who it was, but I still think it was a murder and no accident." She kissed Myles, then headed for the stairs. "Well, I have a ton of shopping to do tomorrow, so I'd better get back to the hotel. I suppose I'll have to walk to Sixth Avenue to get a cab?"

"Probably. I'll go with you."

Paula kissed her good-bye, then started picking up the tree ornament boxes. She wondered what had really happened on that Swiss mountainside twenty years before and felt irritated that her husband would be such a spineless writer as to leave out any mention of the incident merely to avoid offending Duncan Ely.

She also wondered if the pianist had had a dog like Robin twenty years ago.

It wasn't a white Christmas; it was a gray one: gray, chilly and windy as if snow were waiting offstage. But Abby couldn't have cared less. She had been up at six, pulling her sleepy parents out of bed and chattering excitedly as she ran upstairs, plugged in the tree and started opening her presents. At ten her friends started arriving, bringing new presents and excitement. First, George and Myra Schulman with their twin sons, Bob and Ron; then Maggie and Chuck, with their three Indians; then Len DiSilvio with his eight-year-old monster, Barbara, who promptly got in a fight with Abby; finally the Riggs, with Jimmy and Ann, their eight- and ten-year-olds. By the time Janet arrived, children were running all over the two floors.

"My God, it's like a kindergarten—or a zoo!" she said, sidestepping Ron Schulman as he raced down the stairs in an Indian warbonnet, carrying an awesomely realistic machine gun in one hand and a plastic statue of Kharis, the mummy, in the other.

"Zoo's more like it," groaned Paula, hurrying back upstairs to ready the hot cocoa and cookies. "I must be a masochist to do this."

The noise level was higher than a discotheque's, but it lowered considerably as the food was served. Barbara DiSilvio had just shoved a cookie down the back of Abby's dress when the front door buzzed.

"I thought everyone was here," said Myles.

"Darling, you get this one. I got the last."

Myles hurried down the two flights. A minute later, he reappeared, followed by Duncan and Roxanne, their arms filled with packages.

"Merry Christmas!" roared Duncan, in his best Santa style. "Merry, merry, merry, deck the halls, and so forth. Myles, this big green one's for you—"

"And, Paula, this blue one's for you," said Roxanne, handing her a small package, the turquoise paper of which Paula recognized as Tiffany's.

"Abby, here's five packages for you," said Duncan.

"Five?" squealed Abby, her eyes as big as the dogs' in "The Tinder Box."

"Five! Old Santa told me you'd been such a good girl, he was bringing you five! What do you think of that?"

Abby's thoughts were vividly expressed by the ecstatic speed with which she opened the F. A. O. Schwartz toys. Myles whooped with delight as he unwrapped the Artur Schnabel edition of the thirty-two Beethoven sonatas.

"How did you know I've always wanted these?" he said.

"Every pianist wants them," said Duncan. "No one knew those sonatas like Artur. And last time I was here, I noticed they were conspicuously absent. You see? I don't miss much. Paula? You haven't opened your present."

Paula was desperately trying to think of something she could quickly wrap for Duncan and Roxanne, since it had never occurred to her to buy them anything. Now she feigned a smile and opened the gift. It was an exquisite circular brooch in beaten gold.

"Oh, it's lovely!"

"I know it's against the rules for a near-stranger like myself to buy another man's wife jewelry, but when you reach my age you start breaking the rules. And who's this charming lady with the Florida tan? Myles' mother?"

As Myles introduced them to everyone, Paula took Roxanne's sable coat and hurried downstairs with Maggie.

"What can I give them?" she whispered. "I never even thought about it."

"Wrap up the art book Chuck and I gave you."

"I will not! It's beautiful, and Andrew Wyeth's my favorite painter."

"You can buy another later. The point is, it's expensive

and you haven't got time to quibble. Thank God I didn't write in it. Did you ever see such a gorgeous sable?" She ran her hand over the beautifully worked pelts as Paula laid it on their bed. "I think I'll steal it—"

"Did you ever see such a gorgeous woman as Roxanne?" said Paula, adding dryly, "I wish you'd steal *her*."

"Why?"

"I don't like her. Or her father, for that matter." She pulled some gold wrapping paper and red ribbon from her closet and started to cut a sheet. Maggie looked at her with surprise.

"Why don't you like them? They seem perfectly charming to me."

Paula shrugged.

"I don't know. It's just that they're too friendly, I suppose. Too gushy. Call me a cynic, but I don't trust people who are suddenly all over you for no good reason."

Maggie grinned.

"I know why you don't like her. You're afraid she'll steal away that sexy husband of yours."

Paula looked up from her wrapping.

"That's a sweet thing to say."

"Oh, well, don't get all hot under the collar. I don't blame you for being jealous of her."

"I'm *not* jealous of her!" snapped Paula. "It's just that I don't like their snooping."

Maggie shrugged.

"Have it your way. Anyway, I'd like to get her as a customer. I bet she could bring us a lot of chi-chi clients."

Paula dropped the conversation. She finished wrapping the large art book, then hastily scribbled a card and stuck it in the ribbon. Then, looking nonchalant, the two returned upstairs where Duncan was banging out "Jingle Bells" for the kids, who were swarming around the piano singing at the top of their lungs. Paula handed the package to Roxanne, who opened it. She seemed genuinely delighted with the book.

"Duncan and I *love* Wyeth!" she enthused. (I can't stand people who call their parents by their first name, thought Paula.) "His paintings always seem to have such a mysterious quality to them," continued Roxanne, "as if those houses he paints had some magical secret inside them."

"I've always thought that too," said Paula. (Magical secrets. Like you, Roxanne. What's your magical secret?)

"Play something by the Beatles!" yelled Abby. Duncan obligingly played, "Yesterday." The kids loved it.

"Play Christmas carols!" yelled Barbara DiSilvio.

"Yes, Christmas carols!" chorused the others.

Duncan stood up.

"No more for today, children."

"Oh, *please?*"

"Just *one* carol?"

"I already played 'Jingle Bells.' "

"That's not a carol, that's a song."

" 'O Come, All Ye Faithful'? Please?"

"Yes, 'O Come, All Ye Faithful'!"

The kids were jumping up and down, making a terrific racket. To Paula's surprise, a cold expression came over the master showman's avuncular face.

"I said *no.*"

Silence, as the children realized something was wrong. They stepped back, allowing him to leave the piano. Barbara DiSilvio surreptitiously stuck out her tongue at his back. But by the time he had come up to Paula and Janet, the coldness had vanished and he was smiling again.

"That piano!" he said, distastefully. "How can you allow a man with Myles' talent to play on an instrument like that?"

Janet looked embarrassed.

"I know it's terrible, but my son doesn't play anymore."

"He should, he should! He's a terrific musician, take my word for it. Those hands! There aren't a hundred pair of hands like that in a generation."

Janet started to preen herself.

"Yes, they are marvelous hands, aren't they? I can remember when he was a little boy how I used to listen to him play and think, My, how can anyone that young play so beautifully?"

Since Paula knew Myles' mother, given the opening, could gush about her son for hours, she got up to help the other mothers get the children's coats on.

At least he doesn't have to play grand inquisitor with Janet, thought Paula. She'll tell him everything she knows on her own.

Maggie and Chuck were the last to leave.

"Why wouldn't he play Christmas carols?" whispered Maggie as she kissed Paula.

"Don't ask me. Maybe he's Scrooge in disguise."

"It certainly was strange. The kids were loving his playing, and then suddenly—zap! Oh, well, chalk it up to artistic temperament, I suppose. Bye-bye. Happy Hanukkah and all that."

"Good-bye. And thanks for the presents."

She kissed Chuck and the three kids, then started back upstairs. When she reached the living room, Janet was saying, "And when he was eight, mind you, he was playing the 'Appassionata' and most of the really difficult Chopin études. Everybody said he was an absolute genius!"

Even Duncan, the grand inquisitor, looked bored.

Janet flew back to Florida the day after Christmas, eyeing the clouded sky nervously, swearing she should take a bus and filling herself with tranquilizers. After she left, life seemed to return to normal; but Paula knew it hadn't. Duncan Ely's repeated invasions of her privacy, as she considered his unannounced visits, had subtly altered the rhythm of her existence, and she couldn't rid herself of an unnerving sense of foreboding. She didn't know what it was she feared; certainly there was no rational basis for her feeling, for neither Duncan nor Roxanne had done anything that could be interpreted in any way as menacing. As Myles had said, they were only being friendly. Yet Paula felt there was more to it. Perhaps there was a sexual basis to their friendliness. Perhaps the story Janet had told of Duncan's wife's "murder" twenty years before was what was bothering her. Whatever it was, she tried to force her apprehensions out of her mind. She said nothing more to Myles about Duncan. She continued the normal routine of her life.

But the feeling persisted, and it began to affect her sleep. She found that her nights, which were normally untroubled, were beginning to be interrupted by dreams. She couldn't remember the dreams; she would wake up at three in the morning, aware she had had some sort of nightmare but unable to recall any details. She would smoke a cigarette and eventually calm down to the point where she could fall asleep again. But the experience bothered her and heightened her sense of uneasiness.

She found her anxiety was beginning to show in her

face. Two days before New Year's Eve, she took Abby to Chuck van Arsdale's office for a flu shot. Chuck was a homely man with a pockmarked face and a balding scalp who had the reputation of being one of the best young heart specialists in New York. He was on the staff of St. Vincent's Hospital, but because of his friendship with the Clarksons, he served as their family doctor. Paula loved Chuck. He was one of the kindest men she knew; and she felt she was lucky to have this friendly, gentle man as Abby's doctor instead of a coldly impersonal stranger.

When she brought Abby into Chuck's office in the hospital, he took one look at her and said, "Paula, what in the world's the matter with you?"

"Do I look that bad?"

"You don't look good."

She told him she'd been having trouble sleeping but didn't mention the reason. He offered to prescribe some sleeping pills. Paula was tempted but decided against it, since she had no desire to become dependent on barbiturates. More to the point, she knew that pills would not remove the cause of her dreams.

But the fact that Chuck had noticed something made her feel even more unnerved and forced her to admit that her anxiety about Duncan Ely and his daughter had ceased to be a mere annoyance. As she walked out of the hospital with Abby, she faced the uncomfortable fact that Duncan and Roxanne were becoming an obsession with her.

The old year made its exit under a blanket of clear, bitterly cold Canadian air and the threat of another subway strike. Myles and Paula taxied uptown to Sixty-third Street and were ushered inside the gaily lighted town house by Bennet. The first thing Paula noticed was that Duncan was thinner than a week before. He seemed tired and quite a bit older, and though he greeted them with his usual charm, some of his bounce seemed to be gone. She wondered if he, too, was losing sleep.

The house was packed with at least sixty guests. Paula spotted Princess Ina Andrassy, Philip Rosen and a number of musical celebrities, television personalities and *Social Register* names. It was a glittering crowd, and the Louis Roederer Cristal champagne was so superb that Paula broke her sherry habit to have a glass. Duncan led them through the throng to a short man with a beaming red face.

"Sydney, here's the hot young author I told you about," said Duncan. "Sydney Raymont, Myles and Paula Clarkson."

The famous publisher shook their hands. Paula thought that this Goliath of the book world looked in person more like a chubby little David.

"Duncan's been touting you to the skies," he said to Myles. "He tells me you're working on a great novel, something like *The Forsyte Saga*—though I hate *The Forsyte Saga*. When do you think it'll be done?"

"With luck, in four months. My wife's been chewing my ear because I've been practicing the piano instead of working on it."

Sydney looked at Paula.

"Writers' wives, the bane of the profession. Well, Mrs. Writer, I hope you'll let me have first crack at your husband's magnum opus?"

"Of course," she said. "We'd love to have you read it."

Why not? she thought. It was pointless to refuse him now. The time for her to take a moral stand had long since passed.

"I like the idea of an old-fashioned novel," continued Sydney. "Everybody's writing pornography now, but I think there's a limited market for that stuff. Some day the pornie boys are going to find no one's interested anymore. Sex can get pretty dull after a while."

"Perhaps to you, but not to me," said Duncan.

"You old goat!" Sydney Raymont laughed and took a new glass of champagne from a passing waiter. "Well, do you think Lindsay can keep the subways running, or do you think the city's in for another fiasco like two years ago?"

"This city's a permanent fiasco," said Myles. "You can't govern New York. At best, it's nothing but organized anarchy."

"Which is why it's such an exciting place to live," said Sydney.

Roxanne came up to Paula, who had found a seat by the Giacometti sculptures. She was wearing a maroon Empire gown that Paula appraised professionally at about a thousand dollars. There was no denying the woman had excellent taste.

"I wanted to tell you how charming I thought your house was," she said. "You've done a beautiful job on it."

"Thank you." (I wonder if Maggie was right, she thought. I wonder if I *am* jealous of her? God, I hope not! If there's anything I hate, it's jealous women.)

"And your daughter is darling! She's so pretty and full of life."

"She's full of mischef, I'm afraid."

"But aren't all children? I thought she looked a lot like her father."

"Yes, there's a close resemblance."

"You know, I'm an amateur sculptress—"

"Oh, really?"

"Yes, I have a studio on the top floor."

"Do you do modern things like this?" She nodded toward the Giacomettis.

"No, I'm afraid I'm terribly square. I do portrait work, mostly. And I was wondering if your husband would mind doing me a favor? You see, I do life masks—I have quite a collection of them upstairs in the library—and I think Myles has such an interesting face I'd love to make one of him. But I rather hate to ask him, because it takes a good deal of time for the plaster to set, and it's terribly uncomfortable for the sitter."

Paula stared at her, trying to conceal her dislike and her annoyance at the idea of Myles becoming her sitter.

"Well, I imagine Myles wouldn't mind. Do you want me to ask him?"

"Oh, no, I'll do it. But I thought I'd ask you first."

Smiling prettily, she headed toward Myles, who was by the pianos talking to Duncan.

Paula watched her go, thinking, Keep cool, Paula—keep cool. Don't make a fuss about this. If Roxanne's going to try something with Myles, there's no way you can stop her. You just have to trust Myles. He loves you, so keep cool.

Feeling miserable, she took another glass of champagne, keeping her eyes glued on the beautiful creature as she joined her husband and began talking to him.

Myles did better on the "Italian Concerto" than he had done on the Mozart two weeks before, but his perfor-

mance was less than inspired. Duncan of course played well,
but his tone seemed weak, and after the performance he
looked exhausted. However, the crowd applauded enthusiastically, and when Myles joined Paula in the corner, he
looked excited.

"What did you think of that?"

"It sounded very good."

He frowned.

"Don't get carried away. You might accidentally com-
pliment me."

"I'm sorry."

"What's wrong? You look like Bette Davis in *All About
Eve.*"

"It's nothing. Really. I've just got a slight headache."

She tried to smile but made a bad job of it.

"Roxanne wants me to pose for some sort of mask."

"Yes, she told me. Are you going to do it?"

"Why not? I think it'd be sort of kicky being immortal-
ized in plaster. To make a God-awful joke, it'll be the first
time I ever got plastered without having a hangover."

Paula rolled her eyes.

"And on *that* one, I think I'll go upstairs to the john."

She started threading her way through the crowd toward the entrance hall, feeling the beginning of a real
headache. She was disappointed Myles had accepted Roxanne's offer, but she told herself she was foolish to have
hoped he'd refuse. Why shouldn't he? It was an innocent
enough request on Roxanne's part. Everything they did
seemed innocent enough. Why couldn't she rid herself of
the idea they weren't innocent? That they were playing
some elegant game, the end of which would be—what?
Frightening? Yes, that was it. Frightening.

But what was the game?

She came out into the hall and climbed the stairs to the
second floor. The large hallway at the top of the stairs was
papered in beautiful off-white silk, and the modern flavor
of the living room here gave way to antiques. There was a
French *bombé* chest along the wall with a Louis Quinze
mirror above it. Checking her reflection and wishing she
were as beautiful as Roxanne instead of just "pretty," she
walked down the hallway toward the front of the house
where a guest room and bath were being used as a powder
room. The second floor seemed blissfully peaceful after
the noise of the crowd downstairs, and as she reached the

guest room door she was glad to feel her slight headache
was receding.

Across the hall from the guest room was the library.
Paula noticed a number of white masks hanging on the
wall of the room, and remembering Roxanne's mention of
her "collection," she decided to take a look at it. The
room was small but elegant, being lined on three sides
with seven-foot walnut cases fronted with delicate bronze
grillework. The fourth wall contained a large window overlooking the street, in front of which was a beautiful Empire desk with a Directoire lamp on it. Beside the lamp
was an odd assortment of bibelots including a crystal obe-
lisk, a handsome silver inkwell, and a long and quite dead-
ly-looking letter opener with a curiously carved ivory handle that terminated in a grinning death's head. Thinking it
was a rather macabre thing to open letters with, she
looked up at the walls above the bookcases. They were
papered in deep red velvet. On them were hung at least a
dozen of the plaster masks. They were all friends of Duncan; among them she recognized the faces of Sydney Raymont, Philip Rosen, Princess Andrassy and Dame Agatha
Renfrew. There was also a mask of Duncan, and beside it
one of Roxanne herself. The masks were perfect like-
nesses, and in the soft light of the desk lamp they seemed
to Paula almost alive, like a gallery of sleeping heads.

Shuddering slightly, she wandered around the room
looking at the books. Duncan was obviously a voracious
reader with catholic taste: the volumes ranged from biog-
raphies, histories and heavy books on counterpoint and
music theory to cookbooks, books on wine, the latest best
sellers, mysteries and, of course, all the James Bond books
—the latter looking well thumbed. One shelf in the corner
was filled with a number of exquisite porcelain figurines
and objets d'art illuminated by a concealed light and protected by two grilled doors. Paula stopped to admire them.
They were two miniature Chinese dogs, a tiny French
shepherd and shepherdess, and several Meissen figures
Paula knew were probably priceless. In the center of the
shelf was an odd, white porcelain phial, about six inches
high, with a round bottom and a tall, thin neck. Around it
were painted in fine detail a series of grotesque Gorgon
heads, the faces contorted into howls of fury, the snaky
locks joining the heads to form an encircling band. Paula
had never seen anything so hideous, and yet at the same

time so beautifully crafted. It held an almost hypnotic fascination for her, and for a while she couldn't take her eyes off it. Wishing to take a closer look, she tried to open one of the doors. To her disappointment, they were locked.

She turned and saw Robin standing in the library door.

The sight of the big dog staring at her with his coal-black eyes shocked her. She tensed, afraid to move, for a moment certain the animal was going to attack her. Saint Moritz. "Her throat was torn out." Paw prints. That's crazy! she thought. *Crazy!* Labradors aren't killers. Robin couldn't have killed Duncan's wife anyway. That happened twenty years ago, and this dog couldn't be more than three years old. But why doesn't he *move?* Why is he staring at me?

Cautiously, she started toward the dog. He growled. Again, she froze.

For almost half a minute they stared at each other. Then the animal turned around and disappeared into the hallway.

She wanted to laugh with relief. As she hurried across the hall into the guest room, she told herself she had to rid her mind of her wild imaginings. Murder; Roxanne and Duncan's wanting something from Myles; her feeling that there was something evil in this house; these were all sick fantasies she could no longer afford not to fight. It was dangerous to give in to these fears, to be terrified by a Labrador retriever, the gentlest and most harmless dog that existed.

She nodded to the maid in the guest room, walked around the big four-poster bed and went into the bathroom. As she closed the door, she was ashamed to find her hands were trembling.

5

On the first business day of the New Year, Mrs. Lola Mainwaring and Princess Ina Andrassy came into the Beach Bum and bought more than two hundred dollars' worth of clothes. They said Roxanne de Lancre had praised the store so highly, they wanted to see for themselves what she was so excited about.

When they left, Maggie was ecstatic.

"Do you know what this means, Paula? It means we're going to get the in crowd! Oh, that beautiful Roxanne! I love her!"

Paula didn't share her excitement.

Roxanne's trying to bribe me, she thought. She knows I'm suspicious of something, and she's trying to shut me up by sending the store business. . . . Oh, *God!* I've got to stop this!

When Myles returned from Roxanne's studio the following Thursday night, his face was red.

"You sit for two hours with plaster on your face, and you'll look red too," he said as he poured himself a cup of coffee from the Chemex.

"What's her studio like?" asked Paula.

"It's just a big room on the top floor. Nothing fancy. And you'll be relieved to know that Theda Bara didn't try and vamp me."

He sat down at the round table and stirred the coffee. Paula came over and kissed him.

"All right, I was wrong," she said, softly. "And I've been trying not to be jealous, although I haven't done too good a job."

"I can guarantee you don't have to worry about them any more. The reason Duncan and Roxanne have been 'all over us,' as you put it, has nothing to do with sex—straight or crooked."

"What do you mean?"

"Roxanne told me the whole story tonight."

Paula stood beside him.

"What is it?"

"Duncan Ely is dying."

"Oh, no!"

"Oh, yes. They've known it for about seven weeks. He has leukemia. Roxanne said he hasn't got a prayer."

"Oh, Myles, I'm so sorry—"

"I'll bet."

"No, I really am! I had no idea. Though I did notice he looked thinner New Year's Eve."

"He's been refusing to go to bed, I suppose because he knows he'll never get out of it. But yesterday he was so weak he couldn't get up, so Roxanne's hired round-the-clock nurses, and the second floor's been turned into a veritable hospital."

"But why doesn't she send him to a real hospital?"

"He refuses to go. He says he wants to die in his own bed."

Paula felt a surge of pity for the old man.

"Anyway, that's why he took such a sudden interest in me. Roxanne said he's always wanted a son he could pass on his musical talent to—Roxanne got none of it—and so when I met him at the interview and he found out I played, I guess he started thinking of me as his son. It gave him a new interest and something to take his mind off his sickness. And I suppose it was a sort of wish fulfillment for him."

Paula couldn't help but feel relieved at this prosaic explanation of what had baffled her for so long. At the same time, she felt an acute sense of guilt for having been so antagonistic toward the old man and his daughter.

"God, I feel so ashamed."

"Why?"

"I've been thinking all these terrible things about him and Roxanne, and all the time all he wanted was a little love or something. And me sitting down here thinking he was either a sex fiend or murderer!"

"A murderer?"

"Well, you know. His wife."

"Paulie, you didn't believe that crazy story Mother told?"

"I don't know *what* I believed. Except New Year's Eve when I went upstairs I saw Robin staring at me—"

"So what?"

"Well, I had this crazy idea he was going to attack me or something and that maybe Duncan had trained a killer dog to murder his wife."

"For Christ's sake!"

"I know, it was nutty. But I was so bugged by their being nice to us, I started dreaming up all sorts of things. And all it was was—"

She felt like crying. Instead, she leaned down and hugged her husband.

"Myles, don't *you* ever die!"

He kissed her.

"I'm not planning to for a while. Come on now, let's not get carried away. After all, he's lived a good life."

She stood up and brushed back her hair.

"I know. But I don't feel very proud about my behavior. Is there anything we can do for him or Roxanne?"

"I told her to let us know if there was. She's pretty broken up about it. I guess he's in a lot of pain, poor guy. She did ask me to recall the article."

"Why?"

"Because if they accepted it, it would be coming out about the time—you know. So she suggested I wait, and then redo it. Perhaps as a sort of retrospective type thing."

"I suppose that would be better. You know what? I think my whole obsession was all based on jealousy."

"Of Roxanne?"

"Yes. Isn't that disgusting?"

He smiled.

"I don't know. I'm glad you were jealous."

"I had the feeling that somehow they were trying to take you away from me. I guess maybe I'm not as secure as I thought."

"Who's really secure? Nobody."

"I suppose. I guess nobody really knows what's going to happen to them, do they?"

Myles looked at her.

"Duncan Ely knows," he said quietly.

*

He died at midnight on February second.

That afternoon, Myles received a call from Roxanne asking him if he could possibly come up to the house. She sounded exhausted. "What's your blood type?" she asked.

"O positive."

"Good. We may ask you to donate some. They're giving Duncan massive transfusions, though all it is is a delaying tactic. Would you mind?"

"Of course not. I'll be right up."

He called Paula, who said she would come home early to take care of Abby. Then he taxied uptown.

He was met at the door by Bennet, who took him into the living room. Five minutes later, Roxanne came in. She looked as exhausted as she had sounded.

"He's in a coma," she said, "and Dr. Rand doesn't think he's going to come out of it. He's furious at me for not letting them take Duncan to the hospital, but I didn't see the point of it. He didn't want to go, and it's not as if they can save him there. Do you think I was wrong?"

"No. Hospitals are so damned impersonal. I think it's cruel to force people to go there and become a number at the one time they really need to have friends around."

"That's what I think, too. If you meant it about giving some blood, we'd like to take it as soon as possible."

She led him upstairs to the guest room, where he rolled up his sleeve and lay down on the bed. One of the two nurses came in and took a pint of blood. Afterward, Roxanne closed the curtains and said, "I have some hot bouillon for you. Drink it, then lie down for a while. You'll feel weak for an hour or so."

He drank the soup, which was delicious. Then he lay back on the soft four-poster bed. Roxanne looked at him.

"Are you all right?"

"Yes, fine."

"Take a nap. If Duncan comes out of the coma, I'll wake you up. I know he wants to say good-bye to you."

"Yes, do that."

"Good-bye, Myles."

She had said it softly as she closed the door. It had seemed to him a strange thing to say; but he was feeling so drowsy, he quickly forgot it. Turning over on his right side, he went to sleep.

He dreamed he was playing at Carnegie Hall. He was terrified. His hands were sweating. He sat down at the huge piano and started playing the "Mephisto Waltz." To his horror, blood began oozing out of the keyboard, spilling over the piano onto the floor. As the blood started to rise over his ankles, he heard Roxanne's voice saying, "Get out! All of you—get out!" A man argued with her, but she yelled at him again to get out. Her voice seemed shrill, furious—completely unlike her usual low, calm tone.

Now he seemed to be floating in some void. Carnegie Hall and the blood vanished. Then he was back in the guest room, except it had changed. Its proportions were reversed, so that he himself and everything near him seemed small, while the wall opposite him and the highboy against it seemed immense. Roxanne came into the room and looked down at him. She was holding the white life mask she had made of him. She stood over him a moment, then turned and left the room.

A distant clock chimed seven.

Duncan came out of his coma at quarter till midnight. He was in his big bed in the room that took up the rear of the second floor of the town house. The room was luxurious, furnished in modern style like the living room; above the chrome headboard of the bed hung an enormous Daliesque painting, a surrealistic dreamscape stretching to a distant seashore. A tiny figure of a nude woman stood in the foreground of the painting staring at a huge hairy hand that rose out of the far-off ocean. The hand held an eyeball.

The room was dark except for two tiny pinpoint spots above the bed that spilled their muted light down on the dying man, softening his face but at the same time increasing its pallor. Roxanne was seated beside the bed, intently watching her father, whose head was propped up by three pillows. When his eyes opened, she reached over and took his hand.

"Did you get rid of the nurses?" he whispered.

"Yes, and Dr. Rand."

"Is it midnight yet?"

"Quarter till."

He closed his eyes again.

"Then it's time."

Roxanne stood up and turned to the small chrome and glass bed table behind her chair. A delicate porcelain cup, decorated with the same Gorgon's head motif as the porcelain phial in the library, stood next to the phone with a matching saucer placed over it. Roxanne's slim hands removed the saucer, then picked up the cup. Placing it on the saucer, she sat on the bed beside her father and held the cup up to his mouth.

"Drink," she whispered.

He didn't open his eyes. As Roxanne tilted the cup, he swallowed its contents in slow sips—so slowly that it was almost five of midnight before he finished.

Roxanne replaced the cup and saucer on the bed table, then picked up Myles' life mask from the floor.

"Are you ready?" she said.

The old man nodded slowly, then began to mumble.

"Ie n'ay rien qui ne soit a toy, O Maitre," he whispered, as Roxanne watched. *"En ton nom Seigneur cette tienne seruante s'oingt, et dois estre quelque iour Diable et maling Esprit comme toy. Venez, O Antecessor. Venez, venez, O Diable. Venez, Prince et Pere. Venez, Dieu."*

When he had finished, Roxanne leaned over the bed and gently placed the life mask over his face. As she finished, a clock chimed midnight.

Myles, in the next room, awoke when the clock began to chime. He tried to sit up, but he felt nauseous and so he remained with his head on the pillow. He remembered the dream vividly, in all of its sickening, weird detail, but he had no idea what it meant. He wished he could shake off his nausea, for he wanted to get out of this house of death and go home.

Then, as the clock chimed the twelfth stroke, the dizziness intensified, sending his mind into a whirling spiral. It was like a drunken "dizzy mattress," except it seemed a thousand times worse. Myles literally hung on to the mattress as the room gyrated. He was certain he would vomit.

Then, suddenly, it stopped.

At five minutes past midnight, he sat up and looked at his hands. He turned them over, inspecting them, stretching the fingers.

He smiled.

The door opened. Roxanne, silhouetted against the hall light, looked in.

Though her face was in shadow, he felt sure she was smiling too.

He got home at one thirty.

Paula was sitting in bed watching *The Last of the Vikings* on the Late Show, drinking a Diet-Rite Cola. He came over and kissed her as he took off his coat.

"How is he?" she said.

"He died at midnight." He plopped on the edge of the bed. "He never came out of his coma. I suppose it's just as well it's over."

"How did Roxanne take it?"

"All right. She was expecting it, of course. I waited till they got the body out of the house."

"Did you give any blood?"

"Yes, but I don't think they used it. It wouldn't have made any difference. The funeral's Monday. We're invited. Do we have to have that damned movie—"

"I'm sorry, darling."

She got out of bed and shut off the TV.

"You look exhausted. Did you get any dinner?"

"I had some soup."

"Want me to fix you something?"

He was looking at her.

"Come here."

She obeyed. He took her hand and pulled her rather forcefully down on his lap. Then he kissed her, hard.

"I guess you're not so exhausted after all," she said, surprised.

He grinned.

"I'm waking up. Let's go to bed."

"But don't you want something to eat?"

"Maybe later. I want you first."

"Myles!"

"Is there something wrong with that?"

"Of course not—"

"Then let's go."

"I must say, people's deaths affect you in a strange way."

He shrugged.

"I'm a necrophile."

She got off his lap, and he started to undress. Paula was surprised to see, as he stepped out of his underwear, that he had an erection.

"You really *are* waking up!"

He took her in his arms and started kissing her, hungrily.

"You'd wake any man up."

His hands went up under her nightgown and began rubbing her breasts. Then they slipped around to her buttocks. There was something fierce about his hunger she had never sensed before.

"Come on, let's lie down."

She got in bed and started to turn off the light.

"Leave it on."

"Why?"

"I like to be able to see you."

She looked surprised. After she had taken off her nightgown, he eased on top of her. His lovemaking was intense, almost furious.

After it was over, he lay down beside her.

"Wow!" she said, half-kiddingly. "You've really got the old steam up tonight. Did Roxanne give you a vitamin pill?"

He chuckled.

"Let's just say I feel rejuvenated."

"I hope to tell you! Cigarette?"

She had taken her TarGard from the bed table and inserted a Viceroy in it. They always had a cigarette after sex.

"I'm stopping."

"Stopping? You're kidding."

"No, I'm not. You should stop, too."

She put down the cigarette, confused.

"You mean you're *really* stopping?"

"I'm really stopping."

"Just like *that?*"

"It's the only way to do it."

"But why now?"

He didn't answer for a moment.

"A man died tonight of cancer. I don't want that to happen to me. Remember, he told us we should stop? Well, I think we should take his advice."

She hesitated, then put the cigarette back in the pack.

"If you're stopping, *I'm* stopping."

"Good."

"Except we've tried this before, and it never worked."

"It'll work this time. Good night. And, Paulie—"

"Yes?"

"I like your body."

His eyes were closed.

"What a weird thing to say!"

He smiled slightly.

"What's so weird about a husband telling his wife she pleases him?"

She watched him, not knowing what to answer. Within two minutes, he was sound asleep.

She wondered why he didn't turn over on his right side.

Part II

1

Duncan Ely's funeral was held in the chapel of a mortuary on Madison Avenue. As Roxanne said to Paula and Myles when they filed inside the plain, modern room, "Duncan wanted a nondenominational service. His religious beliefs were unconventional."

"Was he an agnostic?"

"Oh, no. He definitely believed. But he didn't believe in any established church."

There were too many people at the service for all to have seats, so the back of the room was packed with standees. Roxanne was the only relative. To Paula's surprise, she and Myles were asked to sit next to Roxanne during the service. Philip Rosen sat next to Paula. She thought that he took the death of his most important client and best friend with unusual equanimity.

A brief eulogy was read by Sydney Raymont, who spoke of "the superlative artistry" of Duncan which would be his "best memorial." No hymns were sung. Paula remembered Duncan's apparent aversion to Christmas carols and wondered if his "unconventional" religious beliefs extended to a ban on all conventional religious music.

The cortege filed under the East River to Queens, then out the Long Island Expressway to a commercial cemetery near Syosset. There, as the crowd of about fifty friends

stood silently around the grave, Duncan's coffin was lowered into the ground without any ceremony. When it had
settled, Roxanne solemnly walked to the edge of the grave
and pulled something from her purse. It was the small
porcelain phial Paula had seen in the bookcase of Duncan's library. She watched with surprise as Roxanne pulled
the stopper from the long neck of the phial, then tilted it
and poured what looked like a clear oil onto the coffin.
Lowering her head, she closed her eyes and mumbled a
few words which were inaudible to Paula. The prayer, if
that's what it was, was brief. Then she put the phial back in
her purse and started for the limousine.

"What in the world was *that* about?" whispered Paula
to Myles as they walked across the grass to their rented
car.

"Don't ask me. Part of his 'unconventional' religious
beliefs, I guess."

"It certainly *was* unconventional! Do you suppose he
was a Rosicrucian or something?"

Myles shot her a cool look.

"Whatever he was, it's none of our business, is it?"

Rather surprised at her husband's curt remark, Paula
climbed into the car and closed the door. As she waited
for Myles to get in, she looked back to the grave. The
crowd had dispersed, but a young man in a black suit and
a black Derby hat whom she had not noticed before was
standing beside the hole. He, too, was emptying the contents of a small phial onto the coffin.

As she watched him curiously, he looked up and returned her stare. Though he was more than thirty feet
away, she felt there was something unpleasant about his
eyes.

She was relieved when Myles pulled the car into the
drive and started back to town.

Roxanne had invited Duncan's friends to a lunch at the
town house after the service.

"If I were Irish," she said as they started up the steps of
the brownstone, "I'd believe in wakes. If there's anything I
loathe, it's the idea of mourning. I think the living have to
try and pick up their lives as quickly as possible after a
death."

"From what I knew of your father," said Myles, "I think
he'd agree with your attitude."

A buffet luncheon was served. As Paula sat down with her plate, Philip Rosen came up beside her. The bald agent-manager was wearing a dark blue suit with a vest that looked tight. He smelled of pipe tobacco.

"I'd appreciate it if you and your husband could be here tomorrow morning at eleven o'clock," he said. "You see, I was not only Duncan's manager; I was his personal lawyer. And tomorrow I'm going to read the will."

Paula put down her fork.

"The will? But why do you want us?"

He smiled.

"I can't answer any questions now. But please be here."

He moved away, and Paula hurried across the room to her husband, who was leafing through some music on the pianos.

"Myles," she said in a low voice, "Mr. Rosen wants us to come here tomorrow for the reading of the will. Do you think Duncan might have left us something?"

Myles looked up. The news didn't seem to excite him.

"That would be nice."

"Nice? It would be heaven! We could certainly use a little extra cash. How much do you think it might be?"

"How would I know? Maybe five hundred dollars, maybe nothing. Maybe he just wanted to thank us or something. Don't count your windfalls before they hatch."

"I won't, but it's fun to think about. Five hundred! What we could do with five hundred dollars! If we get it will you let me buy a portable dishwasher?"

"You mean you're getting tired of dishpan hands?"

She groaned.

"Oh, no, I love washing dishes in that mini-sink. It's the high point of my day."

The reading of the will was held in the library on the second floor. Bennet led Myles and Paula upstairs to the room, where Philip Rosen got out of his seat behind the Empire desk, smiled and shook their hands.

"You're right on time. Good. Just take a seat. As soon as Roxanne gets here, we'll open the envelope."

They sat down in two armchairs, and Philip went back to the legal papers he was shuffling through. For a while, Paula sat quietly, trying not to get her hopes too high over the possible contents of the will. Then she remembered the funeral. Turning around, she looked at the shelf in the corner that contained the collection of porcelain figurines. There, in its accustomed place in the center, stood the small phial, its grotesque Gorgon heads howling silently from its rounded sides. Again she wondered what possible religious significance it could have, and what odd religion called for the pouring of oil on coffins. She thought of the man in the black Derby hat whose eyes had stared at her from Duncan Ely's graveside. Whatever the religion was, if he were in any way typical of its believers, she decided she wanted nothing to do with it.

She turned around and started to reach for a cigarette; then she glanced at Myles, who was turning the pages of the latest *Newsweek*, and reluctantly beat down her hunger for nicotine. Restlessly, her eyes wandered to the door of the room. She remembered New Year's Eve when she had turned to see Robin standing there. Now her fright seemed silly; but she could remember that then it had seemed unpleasantly real.

She glanced at the bookshelves next to the door. In the second shelf from the bottom was a row of books whose leather bindings indicated they were at least a hundred years old. A few of them appeared even older, as if they dated from the eighteenth century. She squinted her eyes to read the small print on the spines. She just had time to decipher two of the titles when Roxanne came in the room.

"I'm sorry I kept you waiting," she said, taking a seat next to Paula, "but one of Duncan's distant cousins called from Chicago, and I had to tell her all about what had happened. I'd completely forgotten about her, which didn't make it any easier."

"You couldn't be expected to remember everything," said Philip. "Now if we're all ready, I'll open the envelope."

He picked up the opener with the ivory handle and slit the flap of a large Manila envelope.

"Duncan made a will five years ago, but it's superseded by this one which he drew up last New Year's Day. It was witnessed by Bennet, Sydney Raymont and myself." He cleared his throat and started reading. "I, Duncan Mowbray Ely, a resident of the Borough of Manhattan in the City of New York in the State of New York, being of sound mind and disposing memory, do make, publish and declare this my last Will and Testament, hereby revoking any and all Wills and Codicils thereto by me heretofore made. Item One. In recognition of my affection for Myles Clarkson, I give, devise and bequeath to him as his absolute property one of my Steinway pianos and my entire collection of musical scores for his personal enjoyment and use in the hope that he will continue his interest in music, for which I believe he has such an extraordinary talent.

Item Two. Furthermore, I direct that within one week of my decease, my Executors pay to the said Myles Clarkson the sum of fifty thousand dollars cash, such sum to be drawn from my personal checking account. This sum I bequeath to the said Myles Clarkson for his support and maintenance, though it is hoped he will use it to further his musical career if he so chooses."

Paula heard nothing more.

Fifty thousand dollars! Fifty *thousand*—

She looked at Myles. He seemed surprised, but she had the feeling he was pretending—as if he had known but didn't want Paula to know it.

Roxanne had turned and was smiling at her.

She knew too, thought Paula. She knew this was in the will. More than that, she doesn't mind. She's actually glad!

"What say we got to the Plaza and celebrate?" said Myles a half hour later as they came out of the house.

"Celebrate?" exclaimed Paula. "Let's go get out of our minds drunk!"

Twenty minutes later, they were sitting in a corner of the Oak Bar sipping champagne.

"I just can't believe it!" said Paula. "I really can't. Fifty thousand dollars—I mean, he only knew you less than two months!"

"It's really crazy, isn't it? I thought you were stopping smoking."

Paula inhaled hungrily. She hadn't had a cigarette in four days and was having nicotine fits.

"I've got to have one now. To celebrate. I'll stop tomorrow. Oh, Myles, just think what this means! Fifty thousand! I about fell off the chair when he said it! And what amazed me is that Roxanne didn't care. She actually was glad we'd gotten it."

"I don't see what's so amazing about that. After all, she got everything else, which must be about four or five million bucks. What's fifty thousand to her?"

"But the piano and the music must have sentimental value to her. Well, she didn't seem to mind, so I'm certainly not going to feel guilty about it. You knew, didn't you?"

"Knew what?"

"Knew he was leaving you something?"

"I figured he must have, or they wouldn't have told us to come to the reading."

"I know, but you knew before that, didn't you? And you kept it a secret so I'd be surprised. You nut!"

She laughed and refilled her glass. The champagne and the nicotine were making her feel giddy.

"Well, he had hinted to me. But I didn't know it would be this much. I guess he was a lot fonder of me than I thought."

"And to think I disliked him! To think I thought he was a murderer! Oh, Duncan Ely, do I love you *now!*"

She giggled and sipped more bubbly. Myles was looking at her, curiously.

"You thought he was a *what?*"

"Oh, you know. All those crazy theories I was dreaming up to explain why he was being so nice to us. Was I ever wrong."

"But who'd you think he'd murdered?"

Paula looked at him.

"His wife. Don't you remember? I told you I thought maybe he'd trained a killer dog. Or even that Robin had done it. I told you all that."

Myles was frowning.

"Oh, yes. It was such a stupid idea, I guess it slipped my mind."

"It *was* stupid. Myles, just think: we can invest the money at maybe three or four percent, and by the time Abby's ready for college we'll be able to pay all her bills without even blinking. Won't that be marvelous?"

"We don't have to invest all of it. Half will take care of Abby. I think we should use the rest of it for ourselves."

"Doing what?"

Myles grinned.

"For one thing, buying you a dishwasher."

"I won't fight you there. A dishwasher! At last. Talk about heaven!"

"And for another thing, how long's it been since we had a vacation? A real one?"

Paula's eyes widened hopefully.

"Myles, do you think we could?"

"Why not? We deserve it. Not a big one, but you know —maybe ten days in Barbados or somewhere."

"Bermuda! I know it's not so chic anymore, but I love it and it's so near. Let's go to Bermuda!"

"Bermuda it is. Do you think we can leave Abby with Maggie?"

"Couldn't we take her with us?"

"And pull her out of school?"

"I suppose you're right. She can stay with Maggie." She brightened again. "Bermuda! Myles, how soon can we go?"

"As soon as the check comes."

"It can be a second honeymoon for us. Tropic sun, coral beaches. And, God, do I need it!"

Myles refilled her glass with champagne. As she watched the bubbles fizz gaily to the surface of the wine, the leather spines of the books in Duncan's library flashed in her mind. *Sadducismus Triumphatus* by Joseph Glanvil had been one of them; *De la Démonomanie des Sorciers* by Jean Bodin the other. She took a slow sip of the champagne, then said, "Myles, do you think Duncan's 'unconventional' religion might have had something to do with Satanism?"

He looked surprised.

"What makes you say that?"

"Well, I saw two books in his library that looked like they dealt with demonology, and it just occurred to me that maybe he was involved with the occult some way or other. I mean, the weird things that went on at his funeral—"

"Oh, he was interested in it, but I don't think he actually practiced it."

"Interested? What do you mean?"

"You know, it was sort of a hobby. He told me he collected books on it, but it was mostly sort of a joke. He never took it seriously. Who could?"

"I suppose you're right," she said, drinking more of the

champagne. "The little I know about it, it's all pretty silly. But I still wonder what he believed in."

Myles smiled slightly as he raised his glass.

"Judging from his will he believes in me."

"Thank God!" said Paula.

Paula really didn't believe the windfall would actually happen until three days later when Myles called her at the Beach Bum and told her the movers were bringing the piano that afternoon.

"How will they get it in? That piano is so huge—"

"They're going to have to rig it and swing it through the window."

"I'd better come over. Do you think they'll move the upright out for us?"

"We can ask."

When she hung up, Maggie asked, "What piano?"

Paula, not being certain of her good fortune, had kept Duncan's bequest a secret. Now she told Maggie. Her partner gaped.

"Fifty *thousand* dollars?"

Paula nodded.

"Isn't that fabulous? Plus one of his grand pianos and all his music, which Myles says is invaluable because it has all his fingering written in and tempo marks and all that—"

Maggie leaned against the counter.

"Why don't things like that ever happen to me? Oh, darling, I'm so glad for you. . . . That's a big lie: I'm really green with envy, but anyway—"

"And if the money really comes, we're going to Bermuda for ten days."

"Don't tell me any more, I'll get sick. No wonder Myles was being so nice to him."

Paula frowned.

"Myles wasn't buttering him up. Duncan was buttering *Myles* up. He'd always wanted a son, and when he found out he was dying he sort of 'adopted' Myles."

"I didn't mean to imply—"

"Oh, I know. Listen, would you like our upright? It's a bomb of a piano, but maybe your kids would get a kick out of it."

"I'd love it. How much?"

"Nothing."

"Don't be silly—"

"Don't *you*. Take it. It's not worth five dollars." She put on her coat on the way to the door. "Remember, I'm an heiress now—Lady Bountiful, giving out goodies. Shall I have the movers take it over to your place?"

"Okay. I'll call the doorman. And, Paula, thanks! And congratulations, Mrs. Gotrocks."

Paula blew her a kiss, then hurried out onto Bleeker Street.

It's fun to be rich, she thought. Being rich has it all over being poor!

A considerable crowd gathered outside the house to watch as the movers rigged the Steinway, then gingerly raised it to the third-floor window. The huge black case, its legs removed, twirled slowly on its straps. Paula, watching from the sidewalk, expected it to crash at any moment, but the movers knew their business. Within an hour, the Steinway was in place in the top-floor living room, and the upright was on the truck. The men agreed to take it to Maggie's apartment for twenty-five dollars, which Myles paid.

"It fills up the whole room!" wailed Paula as she stared at the grand which had been placed beneath the skylight.

"I know," said Myles, sitting down at it. "But it's worth it. Isn't it a beauty?"

"Just a bit of an improvement over the upright. But I don't know how we can give parties—"

"We'll let the guests sit on the piano, Helen Morgan style." He played a few scales, then attacked the "Black

Key Étude." He made a few mistakes, but he performed surprisingly well.

"You must have been practicing again," said Paula when he'd finished. "That was better than I've ever heard you."

He stood up, stretching his fingers.

"I haven't practiced. My muscles are stiff as hell. It's just that anyone sounds good on a piano like this."

He kneeled down and started opening the five large cartons that had come with the piano. They contained all of Duncan Ely's scores, most of which were quite old. He held up one and leafed through it.

"Brahms' Second Piano Concerto," he said, "with all Duncan's tempi markings and phrasing. He's written on the first page: *Performed at Albert Hall, February, 1923, with Beecham.* Can you imagine? Beecham! These things are priceless."

"I'm surprised he didn't give them to the Juilliard, or someone who could get some use out of them."

"I'll get some use out of them," said Myles, quietly.

The check arrived by certified mail the next Monday morning. Myles deposited all but two thousand dollars in a savings account in his name; the two thousand he put in his checking account. By Wednesday Abby had been left at Maggie's and Myles and Paula were on their way to Bermuda. They stayed at the Elbow Beach. The weather was perfect, and the first day both of them got burned.

"I *always* do it," moaned Paula. "I always stay out too long. Why don't I ever learn?"

"I'll fix you," said Myles. They were standing in the bedroom of their fourth-floor suite overlooking the ocean. Myles came over and unhooked the top of her bathing suit.

"What are you doing, you madman?"

"Rubbing Noxzema on you. You don't want me to get it on your bathing suit, do you?"

She stood still as he gently massaged the Noxzema over her burned shoulders and back. Then he came around and did her face, breasts and belly.

"That's a sexy feeling," she purred. "But why put Noxzema on my breasts? They're not burned."

"Because I like to," he replied. "Now put some on me."

She complied, massaging the cream over his strong arms

and back, then rubbing his muscled chest and belly. When she was done, he took her in his arms and pressed her up against him. Their Noxzema-smeared flesh squished as it contacted. He rubbed his torso around slowly against her breasts. The feeling was inordinately sensuous.

"Myles," she whispered, "that's wild—"

He kissed her, then led her over to the double bed.

"Darling, we'll get Noxzema all over the sheets!"

"That's the hotel's problem. This is our second honeymoon, isn't it?"

He pulled off his bathing suit. As always, she thrilled at the sight of his lean nakedness.

"What a honeymoon!" she said, stepping out of her suit.

When they had made love, she stretched out on the bed, happy.

"Myles?"

"What?"

"May I have a cigarette?"

"No."

"Fink."

She bit her lip, then took a deep breath, which Maggie had told her was the best way to fight off the nicotine urge. After three minutes of deep breathing, the urge subsided.

She began to count. During the past ten days, they had made love at least fifteen times. This was a considerable increase over their normal routine. Paula wasn't complaining: she found Myles' new sexuality and the increased fervor of his lovemaking exciting. But she wondered what had caused the change in him. She decided that the bonanza he had inherited had given him a confidence he had lacked before. She had noticed that in a highly competitive society men's manliness often seemed in direct proportion to their capacity to make money. Of course, the reverse was also true. But in the writing profession it was difficult to make money at the beginning, no matter what the state of one's hormones. Myles had made little money so far. Now, suddenly, he had a large amount of cash. This not only salved his insecurities, she decided, but prodded his libido as well.

She smiled at the idiosyncrasies of the male animal.

"Myles?"

"Yes?"

"I ruv you."

"Beg pardon?"

"I said, 'I *ruv* you.' "

Silence.

"Well?"

He sat up and looked at her.

"What the hell does 'ruv' mean?"

She wondered if he was beginning to lose his memory.

They dined at a romantically candled restaurant outside Hamilton. Paula remembered having loved it ten years before when she and four of her classmates had gone to Bermuda during a spring vacation.

"This place used to have the best cooking on the island," she said as they looked over the large menus. "Also the most expensive," she added, shuddering as she glanced at the hefty prices.

"Who cares what it costs? I'm hungry."

"Okay, Howard Hughes."

"Shall I order for both of us?"

"Oh, Myles, I don't want a *steak*—I want something French and glamorous!"

He looked at her coolly.

"I wasn't going to order a steak."

"You always do—"

He frowned and signaled to the waiter. After inquiring about the chef, who, it turned out, was a Frenchman trained at the Plaza Athénée who had migrated to sunnier climes, Myles ordered a brioche de foie gras with a bottle of Riesling Müller 1963; then a filet de sole Monte Carlo; as an entrée, a gigot d'agneau en croûte accompanied by a bottle of Romanée-Conti 1953; and for dessert, lemon crepes with a bottle of Krug Cuvée.

Paula was staggered.

"Myles, since when—"

"Since when did I get interested in good food?" he interrupted. "Since I stopped smoking. Haven't you noticed how much better food tastes now that your tastebuds aren't all smeared with tar?"

"Yes, but you ordered all that with such finesse!"

He grinned.

"I *did* take two years of French, you know, so I'm not a complete hick. And I've been thinking, Paulie: when we get back to New York, we ought to do something more to that kitchen than just get a dishwasher. I mean, that refrigerator is a menace. And there's no counter room. I think we should put in a whole new kitchen. You know, one that's designed so you can work in it without stumbling over yourself."

"But that would cost a fortune, wouldn't it?"

"Three or four thousand, probably. But it would be worth it. Of course, we'll have to make a deal with the landlord. Like get a five-year lease out of him in return for the money we'll be putting into the place. But I think he'd go along with that. What do you think?"

Paula took a deep breath to combat the nicotine fit she was having.

"Well, I don't know—"

"Wouldn't you like a new kitchen?"

"Of course. But the money—"

"Think of the money we're saving on cigarettes."

"We're not saving *that* much."

"We will eventually. And what we save on cigarettes I think we should invest in good food."

"You always liked my cooking before."

"That's not the point. The point is, why should you be miserable in that miserable kitchen? After all, we should enjoy life, and a big part of life is the kitchen and what comes out of it."

She was red in the face from holding her breath. Now she exhaled.

"I guess you're right. You only live once, don't you?"

He smiled slightly.

"That's right. You only live once."

During the next week they swam, bicycled, golfed, danced, water-skied, skin-dived, made love, ate and got beautifully tanned. Paula had never had so much fun, and she had never seen Myles so active. But two things nagged her. The first was Myles' novel. While she didn't expect him to work on his vacation, she had the feeling he had lost all interest in the book. She couldn't explain the feeling; nevertheless, she was sure her instincts were correct. Myles had gone "dead" on novels before and been too ashamed to tell her. With so much time invested in this novel, she dreaded the thought he had gone dead on it too.

One day, when they were waiting to tee off at the

Mid-Ocean Club, she casually said, "Do you still think you can finish the novel in four months?"

Myles was watching a long drive that an English stock-broker had just made. He turned and looked at Paula blankly.

"The novel? Oh, yes. I think so. Do you want to drive first?"

She said nothing more about it. But she was certain his mind was on something else.

In fact, she thought as she teed up, his mind seems to be on a lot of other things lately.

Which was the second thing that nagged her. Something about her husband was different. There were a lot of little things: like the fact that he no longer turned on his right side before going to sleep, or that he now left the bathroom door open when he was washing or shaving whereas formally he had always closed it. There were bigger things: his increased sexuality and a higher level of energy in everything he did. He had formerly been a rather indolent man, fond of daydreaming. Now he seemed continually on the go, much more enamored of physical activity than before.

But there was something even more marked. It was that his mind seemed suddenly to have closed to her. Before, they had had an easy relationship, an instant communication. Now, somehow, the communication had stopped. They talked, but they didn't communicate.

He's switched to another channel, she thought as she went into a slow backswing, forcing herself to keep her eye on the ball. That's the best way I can describe it. It's not only that his memory's gone horribly bad, but he's somehow switched, mentally. . . . Or is it just that he's so *different?*

She swung the driver down, involuntarily closing her eyes just before it hit. The ball flubbed off the tee and rolled to a stop in front of her left foot.

"Oh, damn! I'll never learn this fool game. Can I have another try?"

"It'll cost you a stroke."

"You're mean."

She teed up again, to the annoyance of the foursome behind them.

I know that's crazy, but he *has* changed. Maybe it's just temporary. God, I hope so!

She swung and smacked the ball. It soared into the air, sliced to the right, sailed over the cliff and plunked into the Atlantic Ocean.

"I hate this game!" she wailed.

I wonder, she thought, I wonder if there's something wrong with his mind? Some sort of tumor, or the beginnings of mental illness or something God-awful like that? No, that couldn't be. He's never looked healthier and he's never been so alive. There couldn't be anything wrong with him.

Or could there?

Oh, God, I'm beginning to brood about him like I brooded about Duncan and Roxanne! I've got to stop it. There's nothing at all wrong with him. Nothing. And if he seems a little different—well, having money makes people different. It's made *me* different.

Besides, I really can't complain about his becoming sexier. I can't complain about that at all.

When they returned to New York, they found they owned a dog: Robin.

Maggie had brought Abby home. She was leading the huge black Labrador on a leather leash.

"Momma! Daddy! Look what Roxanne gave me!"

Paula stared at the dog.

"She gave him to you? When?"

"Two days ago," said Maggie. "She called me up and asked if I thought you'd mind if she gave Abby the dog. She said Abby had told her she wanted one last Christmas, and since Robin was Duncan's dog, she had decided to give him away—"

"But I don't want a dog!" sputtered Paula. "You know that."

Maggie gestured helplessly.

"What could I say to the woman? Abby was jumping up and down saying, 'Let me have him,' and I didn't want to insult Roxanne. I mean, after the piano and the money, I assumed you owed her at least a favor, and she *did* want to get rid of Robin."

"Mommy, he's a nice dog. See?" Abby threw her arms around the Labrador's neck and hugged him. Robin raised his muzzle and tried to lick her face. "See? He's really wonderful, and he doesn't wee-wee on the rug or anything—"

"He *is* housebroken," said Maggie. "Thank God."

I can't stand to have that animal in here, thought Paula, remembering New Year's Eve and the terror she had felt meeting him as she came out of the guest room. She turned to Myles.

"Myles, *you* tell her."

Myles was looking at Robin.

"Tell her what?"

"Tell her you don't want a dog."

Myles rubbed his chin.

"Well, she seems to want him. And since he's here—"

"Myles!"

"There's no need to get excited."

"But you always said the last thing you wanted was a dog—"

"Abby wants him, and I don't see how we can refuse Roxanne."

"But *I* don't want that dog!"

"Why?"

"Because I'm *frightened* of him!"

They all stared at her. She immediately wished she hadn't made the outburst. She looked at Robin. He was wagging his tail and rubbing his nose in Abby's palm. It would have been hard to conceive of a less frightening scene.

Maggie snickered.

"I'm sorry you think it's funny," snapped Paula.

"Darling, I didn't know you were so hung up on dogs. But really, *this* one—"

"You don't understand, Maggie," said Myles. "Paula thinks this is the Hound of the Baskervilles of something—"

"Myles, don't be so damned smart! All right, I'm sorry I made a big fuss, and I'm sorry he frightens me. Keep the dog, I don't care." She started toward the bedroom. "But just keep him away from me."

She went into the room and slammed the door.

Maggie raised her eyebrows.

"What's eating her?"

"Oh, she's tired," said Myles, leaning over to scratch Robin's ears. The dog licked his hands affectionately.

"Tired? After ten days in Bermuda?"

"We whooped it up a lot. And she did more than her fair share of boozing."

"La-dee-dah. The problems of the rich. Well, I'm off. Abby, do you have your suitcase?"

"It's in my bedroom."

"All right. Good-bye, darling. You were a good girl, and I enjoyed having you."

Abby kissed her.

"Thank you, Aunt Maggie."

"Bye, Myles. Good to have you home. I'll let myself out."

After she went downstairs, Abby ran to her father and threw her arms around him.

"Daddy, thanks for letting me keep Robin! I'd have died if Mommy had made me get rid of him!"

Myles squatted down and squeezed his daughter's cheeks affectionately.

"We have to be a little patient with Mommy."

"Why?"

"Well, she's not been feeling well lately."

Abby frowned.

"You mean she's sick?"

"No, not sick. Except sometimes she imagines things, you know, things that aren't real. I mean, like being frightened of Robin, which is silly, isn't it?"

Abby giggled.

"Oh, yes, that's *really* silly. He wouldn't hurt a fly."

"But Mommy thinks he might hurt her, so we have to be very patient with her. Understand?"

"Yes, I think so."

"Good. Now you go unpack. First, give me a kiss."

She hugged him. Then she grabbed Robin's collar and ran to her room with him.

"Come on, Robin. You're going to sleep with me in my bed, and I'm never going to let you out of my sight!"

As Abby and the dog disappeared into her room, Myles went into the bedroom. Paula was unpacking his bag. She gave him a resentful look. He came up to her and put his arms around her.

"Come on, Paulie. Abby's nuts about the dog. We couldn't have said no."

She said nothing, but wiggled out of his arms and placed four of his shirts in his bureau.

He grinned.

"Don't you 'ruv' me anymore?"

She looked up.

"I thought you didn't know what that meant."

He took her in his arms again and kissed her.

"What do you mean, I don't know? I know rots about ruv. And rots about Paurie."

She untensed and lay her head on his shoulder.

"I'm sorry I acted like Lady Macbeth. I guess Robin isn't very scary, is he?"

"He only tears out throats when he's hungry."

Paula shuddered.

"Don't even *kid* about that."

"Solly."

She looked into his eyes and brushed back her blond hair, which seemed several shades lighter against her brown skin. "Myles, you're not mad at me about something, are you?"

"Me? You're the one who just blew up."

"I know, but I'm not talking about that. It's just that, well, ever since you got the money, we don't seem to be on the same wavelength anymore."

He sat down on the bed.

"What do you mean?"

"You're different. Like just now: you've *never* wanted a dog. And suddenly you say, let's keep Robin."

He shrugged.

"Can't a man change his mind? And Abby is all over him, so why hurt her?"

Paula checked the urge to argue with him. There were so many things she wanted to ask him; but she could tell he was definitely off her wavelength now, and to pursue the topic would be futile.

"All right," she said. "It's just me. I'm crazy. Let's drop the whole subject."

"But I don't see what you mean saying I'm different. . . . I'm the same as I've always been, as far as I can tell—"

"Really, it's nothing. Let's forget it. Okay?"

He shot her a curious look.

"Okay."

She smiled, trying to appear good-humored, and continued unpacking.

"All I can say is, I'm glad we're rich. Robin looks like he could eat a case of Alpo a day, and dog food isn't cheap. And the first time he goes on the rug, I hope no one expects *me* to clean it up."

Myles said nothing, but continued watching her.

The next day, he received a call from his agent, Don Croydon. The *Times* Sunday magazine had called and offered three hundred dollars for the interview with Duncan Ely, slightly altered to read as a retrospective. Myles agreed and did the short rewrite. The article was to appear the Sunday after the next.

Paula had never had access to considerable sums of money. Her father had been an executive in an insurance company. They had lived in a comfortable, conservative Hartford suburb and had always seemed well-off. But when her mother died of a stroke, it seemed to break her father's will. He had begun to drink heavily and finally was eased out of his executive position. At the end he became a hopeless drunk. When he died, Paula was shocked to find the former insurance executive had left no insurance: he had drunk up the premiums. When everything was sold, settled and paid, she was left with an estate of five thousand dollars, three thousand of which she had invested in the Beach Bum.

Now, suddenly, everything she touched seemed to turn to gold.

The Beach Bum had become hot. Roxanne's boosting the place to her fashionable friends had made it a conversation piece on the Upper East Side. Maggie's designs were praised as "daring" and "kicky." They were swamped with orders. Their accountant told them they had netted eleven thousand dollars after taxes the previous year, and it was obvious they were going to do much better than that this year.

"That's fifty-five hundred each," said Maggie, "which is over five thou. Now you have no excuse for not opening our branch store."

Paula sighed.

"Maggie, that means we're going to have to hire help and God knows what else. Besides, the rents are astronomical uptown. We'll lose our shirts! Let's make this place go. It's taken us this long to get it on its feet—it's crazy to branch out."

But Maggie persisted. She had found an empty store on Madison and Seventy-fifth. The rent was seven hundred and fifty a month, but it was a "perfect" location. She dragged Paula uptown to see it and showed the sketches she had made for its redecoration.

"But we'll need capital to swing this," said Paula. "It'll take at least three thousand to decorate—probably more —and then we have to buy new stock. . . ."

"I've figured eight thousand, to be on the safe side. I've talked to 'my friend at the Chase,' and he says they'll give us the loan—four thousand each, or we can incorporate, which would probably be better tax-wise. Anyway, our business record's good. And Chuck and Myles both have money in the bank which we can use as collateral."

In the end, Paula gave in. They signed a three-year lease and deposited a month's security and a month's rent.

"You'll have to get the place open," said Paula as they left the landlord's office. "I'll have my hands full with my own carpenters, fixing our kitchen. So I'll run the Bleecker Street shop, which will leave you free to get uptown open." To which Maggie readily agreed.

George Schulman, the father of the twin boys who were Abby's friends, was a young architect whose designs were highly praised but whose fees were so meager as to keep him and his family barely at the subsistence level. Paula hired him to redo their kitchen. "I know it's a piddly little job, George," she had said, "but you know how nuts I am for your designs, and Myles and I would really appreciate it if you could find time to do it."

"Find *time?*" said George "This is the first job I've had in two months. Are you kidding?"

In two hours he had sketched an ingenious design that exploited every square inch of the tiny kitchen. Both Myles and Paula were enthusiastic about his ideas. They badgered their landlord into a new five-year lease in return for the renovation. And two weeks after their return from Bermuda, George brought in his carpenter, Mr. Flower, and his plumber, Mr. Kovak, to begin tearing out the old fixtures.

That night, Myles and Paula joined Maggie and Chuck at the Granados restaurant to celebrate the signing of the loan at the Chase for Beach Bum North, as they had decided to name the uptown store. Myles was in a surly mood.

"What's wrong with you?" asked Chuck. They were sitting at a table near a window looking out on the corner of MacDougal and West Third, which was thronged with tourist, hippies and tourists pretending to be hippies. Chuck had a passion for paella, and he and Maggie frequently ate at the superb Spanish restaurant only two blocks from their apartment building. He loved Sangría, too, which he was pouring out of a tall glass pitcher.

"Noise is wrong with me," growled Myles.

"Noise? What noise? Sonic booms? Traffic noise? Screaming neighbors? What? When you talk about noise in New York, you've got to be specific."

"Kitchen-being-torn-out noise," replied Myles. "Those carpenters drove me bats today, and there's three more weeks of it yet to come. I didn't get a damned thing done."

"I never thought of that," said Paula. "Isn't there any way they can muffle it?"

"Oh, sure. They can put cork on their crowbars."

"Maybe you could wear earplugs?" suggested Maggie.

"Maybe we can rent you a room somewhere for the next three weeks," said Paula.

"You can work in our place if you want," volunteered Chuck. "The maid and Tim are there all day, but they shouldn't bother you."

Myles shook his head.

"Thanks, but I'm a prima donna. I have to be alone to get anything done. And, Paula, I'm not going to sit in some grubby rented room for three weeks. That would drive me crackers."

"Then what'll we do? Should we stop the carpenters?"

"Too late for that. I don't know. Maybe I'll go see three weeks' worth of movies."

They were starting their second pitcher of Sangría when Roxanne came into the restaurant with Philip Rosen. Paula hadn't seen her since the reading of Duncan's will and had almost forgotten how beautiful the woman was. She was wearing her sable coat. Her black hair was pulled back in a chignon, and she looked as if she'd just stepped out of an ad in *Vogue*.

They came over to the table.

"Paula! And Myles! What a surprise to see you here!"

Get off it, thought Paula. You knew we were going to be here tonight.

"We're going to see *House of Flowers* over at the Theatre de Lys and thought we'd have some Sangría first."

"Why don't you join us?" said Chuck.

They did.

"We were just trying to figure out what to do with Myles," said Maggie after the waiter had put them all at a larger table and Philip had ordered. "They're having some work done on their kitchen, and the noise is driving him out of his mind."

Roxanne smiled across the table at Myles.

"There's an easy solution to that. I'm flying to Jamaica tomorrow for a month. Come up and use the town house."

"I couldn't do that," said Myles, unconvincingly.

"Why not? The place will be empty, except for Bennet coming in to clean. You can work in the library, or wherever you want. And I'd prefer having someone there during the day to discourage burglars."

"Well. . . ."

She reached into her purse and pulled out a set of keys.

"Then it's settled. Here's the keys. I'll be out by noon, and then the place is yours."

She handed the keys to Myles, who pocketed them and thanked her profusely.

All arranged, thought Paula. This was all arranged. Myles told her we'd be here tonight for dinner. She comes and gives him the keys in front of me, so it will all look casual and I won't start getting suspicious. . . .

Suspicious of *what*?

I don't know, I don't *know!* Why do I think everything this woman does has some sort of purpose behind it? Why don't I trust Myles anymore? After all, it could be a coincidence they came here tonight. There are eight thousand restaurants in New York, but it *could* be a coincidence. . . .

And what am I afraid of? She's going to in Jamaica, so what do I care if Myles goes up there to work?

As the waiter brought the salad with the tangy dressing in the wooden bowls, another thought occurred to her that made her even more miserable. It had been Myles' idea to redo the kitchen. Could he have suggested it, knowing the noise would give him an excuse to get out of the house? Knowing he could then arrange it with Roxanne to use her town house?

But that's crazy too. Why would he want to use the town house? What's in it that he wants?

She remembered the anxieties and suspicions that had ruined her sleep before Duncan had died and told herself she mustn't fall into that trap again. There was nothing in the town house Myles wanted except peace and quiet. That was all, and she was an idiot to think there was anything more to Roxanne's offer than a gesture of friendship.

Forcing the fantasies out of her mind, she began to eat her salad. But her appetite was gone.

During the next two weeks, Paula was kept so busy she had little time to think about Myles. With Maggie uptown supervising Beach Bum North, Paula had to run the shop alone. The increased business kept her on her feet all day;

and since she had to close up and do the day's accounting
and banking by herself, she seldom got home before eight.
With the kitchen being torn up, they all had to eat out. It
was an exhausting way to live, and Paula prayed for the
day the kitchen would be done.

The only bright spot in this bedlam was the appearance
of Myles' article on Duncan Ely in the *Times* Sunday
magazine. While Myles took his publication in the presti-
gious newspaper matter-of-factly, Paula was thrilled. She
bought ten copies, sent one to Myles' mother in Florida
and filed the others in his workroom. "For your biogra-
pher," she told him. The photographs accompanying the
article included one taken years before of Duncan, Roxanne and William de Lancre, Roxanne's ex-husband. He
was a handsome, dark-haired man, a partner in his father's
blue-chip brokerage house, De Lancre, Reardon and Lord.
He had never remarried after divorcing Roxanne; and the
article ignored the details of the divorce completely. She
asked Myles if he knew what had gone wrong with the
marriage.

He shrugged.

"I guess they just didn't get along," he said.

On the Monday of the third week, she closed the shop
at noon and taxied uptown to see the progress on Beach
Bum North. Maggie had hired and supervised the work-
men herself, and when Paula arrived, four of them were
installing the small dressing rooms in the back. The shop
was not large, but by creating an island in the center
which could hold almost a hundred items, Maggie had
doubled the amount of display space. The decor was to be
psychedelic, and Jimmy Ress, a young far-out artist Maggie knew, was painting wild swirls of color on the ceiling
and walls as a background for a number of Personality
Posters that would be pasted up later. "It'll give us head-
aches," Maggie confessed, "but it'll sure as hell look with-
it." The grand opening was two weeks off, and Maggie had
hired a rock singing group to entertain. "Opening day
we'll be practically a discotheque," she said. "Which
wouldn't be a bad idea. You know, the drugstore next
door is owned by a man who's thinking about retiring. We
might take over his lease and open a discotheque—"

"Maggie!" said Paula.

"Sorry. It was just an idea."

On an impulse, Paula decided she'd drop by and say hello to Myles. Leaving the shop, she hailed a cab and told him to take her to East Sixty-third Street. It was a sparkling day, full of sunshine and the first hint of spring. When she got out of the cab, she climbed the steps of Roxanne's town house and started to ring the bell.

She stopped and listened.

Inside, someone was playing the piano. She recognized the haunting waltz theme and the murky nineteenth-century harmonies of the "Mephisto Waltz." She also recognized the superlative technique, the sensuous tone and the unmistakable style of the pianist.

It was Duncan Ely.

But he's dead! He's *dead!*

She resisted the panic that momentarily gripped her. The music had stopped. Now it picked up again, repeating a few measures more slowly.

He's practicing. . . . Duncan Ely is practicing. . . .

She rang the bell. Again, the music stopped. A minute dragged by. Then the door opened.

Myles smiled at her.

"Paulie! What are you doing here?"

For a moment, she could say nothing, she was so glad to see her husband's face.

"I was looking over the new shop and thought I'd drop by to say hello."

She came into the foyer, and Myles kissed her.

"Have you had lunch?"

"No."

"Why don't we go out and have a hamburger?"

"Isn't there anything in Roxanne's refrigerator we can nibble on?"

Was she mistaken, or did he look nervous for a moment?

"No. The cupboard is bare. Wait a sec: I'll run up and get my coat."

He started toward the stairs.

"Myles?"

"Yes?"

"Who was playing the piano a moment ago?"

"Nobody. Why?"

"But I *heard* it. Outside. Someone was playing the 'Mephisto Waltz.' "

"Oh, that. I had on one of Duncan's tapes he used to

make of himself practicing—you know, so he could listen to himself. There's piles of them here. Be down in a minute."

He hurried up the stairs.

Tapes! Of course, tapes! No ghosts. Or rather, the modern ghosts: the sounds from the past, the voices of the dead.

Tapes.

They went to Phoebe's Whamburger for lunch, but she really wasn't hungry. Again, the doubts, fears and suspicions began to assail her. It was as if a playlet of normality was being performed for her benefit, but behind the smiling masks of the charade something else was going on. Something she sensed but couldn't understand. Was it only her imagination that was nagging her into thinking it was a charade? Was, perhaps, *she* the one that was experiencing the beginning of a mental illness, rather than Myles?

Or was it her woman's intuition that was sensing the truth.

She thought of a way she could find out.

Leaving Myles outside the Whamburger after lunch, she walked to Fifth Avenue and caught a taxi to the Village. She let herself in the house and climbed to the second floor, calling "Hello" upstairs to Mr. Flower, the carpenter, who was putting the last touches on the new kitchen. Then she went into Myles' workroom and opened the desk. There lay the novel manuscript. She picked it up and looked at it. Myles always dated each day's work to keep track of his progress; the last date on the manuscript was February first.

Six weeks ago. Six weeks that he had done nothing on the novel.

Then what was he doing uptown?

The next day, she closed the shop at ten o'clock and again taxied to Sixty-third Street. Now she thought she knew the answer, and the truth—if it were the truth— sickened her. But she knew she had to face it. Face it and either overcome it if she could or, if she couldn't, somehow adjust to it. The ultimate step, divorce, she wouldn't take unless she was forced to. She loved Myles too much to leave him.

But first she had to make sure.

She got out of the cab at the corner of Sixty-third Street and walked down the block till she came to a small antique shop catercorner from Roxanne's house. The shop was in the ground floor of an old town house and was run by a pleasant woman with silver-blue hair. Paula asked her if she could browse. "Of course," smiled the woman. "Take all the time you want. I'll be in the back."

After she had gone, Paula slowly wandered around the shop, never going too far from the front window through which she had an excellent view of the town house across the street.

Twenty minutes had passed when she saw Duncan Ely's black Rolls-Royce pull up in front of the house and park. Bennet was at the wheel in his chauffeur's uniform.

A minute later, the front door opened and Roxanne de Lancre came out of the house. She was wearing a dark mink coat and carrying an alligator bag. She came down the steps to the car. Bennet held the back door open as she climbed in. Then he got in the front, and the car pulled away.

"Have you found anything?" called the woman from the back.

"No. . . . Thank you. Good-bye."

"Good-bye."

Paula left the shop and crossed the street. Her eyes were filling with tears—tears of rage, of hurt, of disappointment. She tried to fight them back. Now she knew why Myles hadn't wanted her to look in the refrigerator. Roxanne's cupboard was far from bare: it was probably full. As full as any refrigerator is when the owner is home instead of in Jamaica.

She climbed the steps of the house. Again, she heard Duncan Ely playing inside, this time a fugue from the Well-Tempered Clavier—brisk, clean, dry, like a good martini.

She rang the bell. The music stopped. A moment later, Myles opened the door.

His surprise, at least, was genuine.

"Paulie!"

She came inside. He closed the door and looked at her.

"What's wrong?"

She went into the living room. He followed her, closing the double doors behind him.

"You look upset."

She looked around the big room, then turned to him.

"Myles, why have you been lying to me?"

"Lying?"

"Please don't give me that innocent little-boy look. You worked this all out with Roxanne, didn't you? The whole business: redoing the kitchen so you'd have an excuse to get out of the house, her meeting us that night at Granados to give you the keys to this place—"

"What are you talking about?"

"Myles, I'm not a fool! Roxanne's not in Jamaica. She never went to Jamaica, and she never intended to go! She's been here all the time! Here with you, while poor dumb Paulie sits downtown—"

"Roxanne is in Round Hill."

"Myles, I just saw her leave the house. Now *stop* it!"

He went to the built-in bar and poured himself a drink. When he finally spoke, his voice was quiet.

"All right, she's been here. And we did plan it. But I haven't been making love to her, if that's what you think."

"That's exactly what I think."

"Then you're wrong."

For a moment, she almost believed him. She wanted to believe him.

"What's been going on, then? You certainly haven't been working on the novel. I checked that, and the last thing you wrote was six weeks ago."

"Do you want a sherry?"

"No. And you shouldn't be drinking in the middle of the day, particularly Scotch. Or is that part of the all-day orgy?"

He leaned on the piano.

"The only orgy that's been going on has been an orgy of practicing."

"Practicing? Oh, come *on*. I may be dumb Paulie, but I'm not a cretin!"

"It's the truth. I've been practicing. Scales. Czerny. Bach. Chopin. Six hours a day, every day."

"But why?"

"Paulie, I'm giving a debut at Carnegie Hall six weeks from now. Philip Rosen's arranged it for me. He's become my manager."

She sat down.

"A debut?"

"A debut. The debut of the new Myles Clarkson."

He came across the room, squatted beside her chair and took her hand.

"Paulie, you know the piano's my first love. It always has been. Okay, I gave it up because I fell on my face. But Duncan gave me new hope—hell, he gave me more than hope, he gave me *money*. Remember what he said in the will? That he hoped I'd use the fifty thousand for my musical career? Well, I think I owe it to him to give it a try. Roxanne and Philip feel the same way. I told them I didn't want you to know until I had time to feel sure. That's why we concocted all these lies and all this complicated business to get me out of the house so I could practice without your knowing. Well, you found out anyway. But it doesn't matter, because Paulie, now I *am* sure! I'm good Paulie! I'm as good as Duncan said I was! I think I'm going to be great in Carnegie Hall, and with Philip managing me and Roxanne making contacts for me, I'm going to have a great career. I can be another Duncan Ely. I can have as exciting a life as he had, and so can you. I've studied his tapes, I've studied his scores—I've learned his style, Paulie, and I'm *good*." He stood up and looked at her. His expression wasn't pleading, nor was it defiant. But there was an enormous strength in his face. "That's the Big Secret. Now that you know it, I hope you'll be with me. But don't try to fight me, Paulie. I intend to give this a try. If I fall on my face, okay. But nobody's going to stop me from trying."

She didn't say anything for a moment. While she was relieved that he was being honest with her at last—or at least, he *seemed* to be—and relieved that he wasn't sleeping with Roxanne—or at least he *claimed* he wasn't—still, she could hardly believe that he was serious about beginning a concert career at the age of thirty-two.

"What happens if you fall on your face?" she finally asked, quietly.

He shrugged.

"Then I can go back to the novel, and what have we lost? Maybe two or three months, and whatever money the debut costs me. But I'm not going to fall on my face. Listen."

He went to the Steinway and sat down. She watched as he studied the keyboard, just as Duncan Ely used to do. Then he attacked. It was the third movement of the

Schubert A Major Sonata, the same sonata Duncan had played that night so long ago. It was obvious from the first few measures that Myles was no longer the sloppy amateur. His tone was full and rich, his technique flawless. The parallel scales rippled with blinding speed; the elegant second theme bubbled with charm and sophistication; the musical conception was masterful. She listened, stunned by the brilliance. At one point, she closed her eyes.

It was exactly as if she were listening to Duncan Ely.

He played for an hour and a half.

He played two Bach preludes and fugues. He played the Mozart "Hornpipe Sonata." He played the first Chopin scherzo, the second Brahms rhapsody and a dazzling Khatchaturian toccata. He finished with the stupefyingly difficult Paganini-Liszt étude, "La Campanella."

When he was through, he stood up, rubbing his hands together.

"Well? Are you impressed?"

She was frightened. She didn't want to show him, but she was frightened. She told him she was impressed. She told him he should try the debut if he wanted: she wouldn't object. She would help him any way she could.

He seemed relieved. He said in that case there was no reason why he couldn't practice at home as soon as the kitchen was finished. She agreed, kissed him, then left the house.

Once out on the street, she took a deep breath of air.

It's impossible, she thought as she walked toward Fifth. No one could get that good in a few weeks' time. No one. Particularly Myles. He hasn't practiced—really practiced —for years. He was never that good even when he *did* practice, years ago. It's impossible. I don't believe it.

And yet, I heard him!

Or did I?

Did I hear him or Duncan Ely?

Was he playing some trick on me? Did he put on Duncan's tapes and just pretend to play, synchronizing his fingers with the notes like actors dub foreign films? But what would the point of it be? Besides, he couldn't have. I saw his fingers: they were doing the playing. There were no tapes.

But he couldn't play that well! And if it wasn't him playing. . . . if it wasn't Myles. . . . Who was it?

Oh, God, who *was* it?

She was too afraid to go back to the store, so she went home and lay down on her bed. Upstairs, the carpenters were hammering, their hammerblows echoing around the house. She tried to crowd the noise out of her mind so she could think. Did she really believe Myles' story? Did she really believe the only thing going on in the town house was his practicing? Or was he making love to Roxanne? She remembered her suspicions before Duncan Ely had died: her certainty that Roxanne was after Myles. Could it be possible that all she was after was his musical talent? Could it be possible her husband wasn't attracted to the beautiful woman, that all he was interested in was her ability to help him carve out a concert career?

And what about that concert career? How could he become so good so quickly? His playing had seemed to be a miracle, but she didn't believe in miracles.

She didn't know what she believed in.

The only thing she knew for certain that she believed was that Myles had changed. So far, she had made up plausible explanations for the differences she had noticed in him. But she couldn't make up a plausible explanation for his sudden brilliance at the keyboard.

She tried to think back, to remember exactly when she had started noticing the changes—the exact moment he had switched to another channel and stopped communicating with her. It had happened before they went to Bermuda. Was it when he found out he had inherited the money? No, it was before that.

She remembered.

It was the night Duncan Ely had died.

It was when Myles had come back from the house and she was watching *The Last of the Vikings* on the Late Show. She reconstructed the scene in her mind. He had come into the bedroom and sat on the edge of the bed. He had told her about waiting till they took Duncan's body out of the house. Then she had said something about whether he had had any dinner and whether he wanted something to eat. . . . And he said he wanted to make love first. Then he had started to undress. . . . Yes, she remembered now. And he had left the light on—that was it! He had never left the light on before when they made love, but that time he had left it on. And his lovemaking had been different —more fierce, more savage. And afterward he told her he was stopping smoking—she remembered now! And then he had made the bizarre remark—he had said, "Paulie, I like your body," or something like that. . . . *As if it had been the first time he had ever made love to her!*

And then. . . . Yes, that was the first night he went to sleep without turning on his right side. . . .

The change in Myles had started the night Duncan Ely had died.

But what did that mean? What could it possibly mean? That Duncan Ely's ghost was haunting him? Or that Duncan Ely had hypnotized him? Or what?

She rolled over on her stomach, burying her face in the white bedspread. She didn't understand. It was like looking through a dense fog and seeing the vague outline of an object, but not being able to tell whether the object was a ship or an iceberg. An iceberg—that was it. Nine-tenths below the surface, one-tenth above. Myles was one-tenth visible—the "normal" Myles, the smiling friendly Myles. But what was below the surface? A Myles that could suddenly play like Duncan Ely?

Like Duncan Ely!

She didn't believe in transmigration of souls, but she had to admit to herself that Myles had somehow become Duncan Ely on the night Ely had died, almost as if Ely's soul had entered Myles' body. That was the only logical explanation to the "new" Myles whose personal habits were so strangely different, whose memory was so strangely bad, whose sexuality was suddenly triple forte and who could play the most difficult pieces in the piano repertoire like a seasoned master.

But of course, that wasn't a logical explanation. It was a completely illogical explanation.

She found herself crying softly. She was confused. But most of all, she was afraid. Afraid, because she didn't know exactly what she was afraid of.

She heard a panting sound beside the bed. She rolled over and looked down. Robin was lying on the floor, his tongue out, panting heavily, watching her.

Her skin crawled. She wanted to scream. She wanted to kill Robin. She wanted Myles back—*her* Myles: daydreaming, lazy but lovable Myles, not this new Myles she didn't know. She wished she had never seen Duncan Ely or Roxanne or this damned hound, Robin. She would gladly give back the fifty thousand dollars if by doing so she could erase all that had happened the past few months since that morning Duncan Ely had called about the interview.

The fifty thousand dollars. . . . The piano. . . . The scores. . . .

If Duncan Ely knew he was going to become Myles Clarkson, wouldn't he will some of his money to Myles? Myles, who would really be Duncan? Wouldn't he? And his piano and his scores too?

She was thinking gibberish. It made no sense at all. People couldn't "take over" other people's bodies. It sounded like something out of *Time Tunnel*, or the Middle Ages—diabolical possession or witchcraft. . . .

Diabolical possession? *De la Démonomanie des Sorciers*. Was it possible that Duncan, Roxanne, Ina Andrassy, Philip Rosen and that strange man in the black Derby hat—was it possible they were all Satanists? And that somehow Duncan and Roxanne had cast a spell that enabled the dying man to possess the younger man's body?

No, no, that was crazy. And even if it were true; even if Duncan, knowing he was going to die, had begun to look for a different body he could take over, why would he pick Myles? Yes, Myles was young and healthy and handsome. But still. . . .

Then she remembered: the hands. The Rachmaninoff hands. "What does that mean, he collects hands?" "There aren't more than a hundred pair of hands like that in a generation." The hands. Of course. A great pianist would want great piano hands. That's why he had picked Myles, studying him and his family so intently so he could "pass" when he transplanted himself. That's why Myles has suddenly decided to become a pianist: because he's not Myles, he's Duncan Ely in a new body, literally handpicked, starting a new career. . . . No, continuing his old career in a new body. . . .

She started to giggle. The idea of going shopping for a new body to take over seemed wildly funny. "Mommy, I'm tired of this body. Let's go down to the body shop and pick out a new one." "Darling, I have a toothache. I'm going out and get a new set of teeth—in a new body." She was rolling over on the bed, laughing hysterically. Why bother with heart transplants? Get yourself a whole new body, it's much easier. *Soul* transplants: that's the ticket. Soul transplants. You never have to die. Wear out one body, take over a new one. You can live forever. Maybe Duncan Ely was ten thousand years old!

There was only one problem: What happened to the soul of the body you took over? What had happened to Myles? The real Myles? Her Myles? The Myles she loved? Was he *dead?*

The hammering upstairs had stopped. Mr. Flower, the carpenter, was running down the stairs into the bedroom where he had heard the scream.

"Mrs. Clarkson, are you all right?"

The old man in the dungarees was staring at her. She sat up, wiping the tears from her face.

"Yes, I. . . . I'm all right."

"I heard you making a lot of noise down here and thought maybe you was sick?"

"Thanks, Mr. Flower. I think I had a nightmare, that's all."

"Oh. Well, it must have been a real spooky one."

"I guess it was. A *real* spooky one."

He went back upstairs.

A nightmare, she thought. A real spooky nightmare. An insane nightmare. Except is it the nightmare that's insane —or me?

By the time Myles came home from Roxanne's that evening, Paula had decided that if she were going to keep her sanity she would have to push the wild fantasies of that afternoon out of her mind. The reality of the situation was that her husband, who at one time had been a mediocre pianist, had suddenly become a great pianist. Call it hard work, call it inspiration—call it anything but black magic. It was a fact. It was a fact he was going to play in Carnegie Hall. It was a fact that if his debut were a flop, he'd return to writing. If it were a success, he'd go on with music. That was all very clear-cut and simple, and any thoughts of "soul transplanting" were sheer drivel.

She would have to control her imagination; but she wondered if she were strong enough to do it.

Three days later, the kitchen was finished.

The cost had gone nine hundred dollars over George Schulman's estimate, but Myles didn't complain. "It's worth it," he said to Paula as they inspected the gleaming new room. "Did you ever think this rathole could look this good?"

George had done an expert job. The new electric range and oven were covered with a shiny copper hood with an exhaust fan inside. Beside it, seeming acres of vinyl counter space stretched around the room with more acres of storage space in the wooden cabinets underneath and above. A light blue refrigerator-freezer stood in the corner, and a gleaming stainless steel double sink with a dishwasher and garbage disposal was installed beneath the window, which held a new air conditioner. A fake Spanish tile linoleum floor had been laid, and from the light blue ceiling hung an antique wrought iron chandelier with two round glass globes over the lights.

Paula wandered around the room, running her fingers lightly over the fixtures and the blue vinyl counters. This is reality, she thought. This kitchen. This refrigerator, the vinyl, the dishwasher. This is reality, and I love it.

She turned and smiled at Myles.

"Darling, I'm going to cook you the best dinner of your life!"

Is he my darling? Or is he some genie or mutant or transplant or whatever. . . . No, no, NO! Reality. The refrigerator. The oven. General Electric. Live totally with total electric living. That's us. We're living totally with total electric living. That is reality.

Myles is Myles. G.E. is G.E. Total electric living is total electric living. A is A. B is B.

Q.E.D.

She opened the new refrigerator, pulled out the plump chicken breasts, and started to make suprêmes de volaille à blanc.

I've got to make sure, she thought. I'm never going to have real peace of mind until I make sure. But how?

She decided to ask him. Point blank. If he were really Myles, and not some reincarnation of Duncan Ely, he wouldn't know what she was talking about. He'd look baffled. A Duncan Ely might be clever enough to fake the bafflement, but she didn't think so. Not if she caught him unawares.

It was as good a way as she could think of.

Yes, she would ask him.

The dinner was a masterpiece. It had been such a joy to be back in her own kitchen—particularly this shiny, brand-new convenient kitchen—that she almost forgot her worries in the pleasure of cooking. She even dug out her files of *Gourmet* magazines, so unused in the former steak-and-potatoes days, and found a recipe for the lemon crepes they had enjoyed so much in Bermuda. They were hard to make, but the delirious reception they received from Myles and Abby made the trouble worthwhile. She further pleased Abby by giving her a scoop of vanilla Häagen-Dazs ice cream on one of the unlemoned crepes.

"What did I tell you?" said Myles as he finished his eighth crepe. "Isn't this new kitchen worth all the mess and expense?"

"Every nickel," said Paula.

"Personally, I think George Schulman did a great job. Someone ought to take a picture of the kitchen for *House and Garden*. You know, one of those 'How We Converted Our Broomcloset into an Extra Bedroom' articles."

"Momma, can I go feed Robin now?" said Abby.

"May I."

"May I?"

"Yes, darling."

"Okay. And it really was a good dinner."

When she left the table, Myles reached over and took Paula's hand.

"Are you still scared of Robin?" he asked, gently.

She hesitated.

"No." What a lie *that* is, she thought.

"Are you still scared of me?"

"You?"

"You seemed scared the other day. At Roxanne's. You know, after I played for you."

"I wasn't scared—"

"You looked it."

All right, she thought. Now's the time to bring it out.

"I guess I was, a little."

"Why?"

"I don't know . . . it came as such a shock to me, your telling me you were going to become a pianist, and then . . . then you played so brilliantly. It just seemed impossible to me you could get that good. It still does, actually."

He moved his chair next to her and put his arm around her.

"Nothing's impossible if you put your mind to it."

"I know. The Power of Positive Thinking and all that

bazazz. But still—I mean, for a moment I thought"—she watched his reaction out of the corner of her eye—"I thought you were Duncan Ely."

No reaction except a grin.

"I am. I told you I was aping his style by studying his tapes. No one plays like Duncan now, and there's a big audience for his bravura-style pianism. I want to cash in on it."

"But I didn't mean that, exactly."

"What did you mean?"

She turned and looked directly into his eyes.

"I meant I was scared because I thought you had become Duncan Ely. That is, well, his 'soul' had gone into your body."

A look of bewilderment.

"Huh?"

Now the terror was gone. He doesn't know what I'm talking about, she thought. Thank God! Unless he's pretending—no, he couldn't be that good an actor. He doesn't know! He is Myles! Myles is Myles! Thank God, thank God!

"What are you trying to say, Paulie? Duncan's soul has gone into *my* body! Have you started to dig yoga or the Maharishi or something?"

Now she was laughing and hugging him and kissing his ears and his cheek and his eyes.

"No, no. . . . It was all this crazy dream I had. Don't pay any attention to me, really don't. I'm just a nut."

"Hey, what was in that chicken? You've gone wild!"

"That's because I'm wildly in love with you, of course. And, Myles?"

"What?"

"I want you to know I'm really behind you. I mean, with the piano business. I'm really behind you, and I know you're going to be great at Carnegie Hall."

He smiled, pulled her onto his lap and kissed her.

Thank God! she thought. The nightmare is over. Thank God.

"Myles?"

"What now?"

"There's *really* nothing going on between you and Roxanne?"

His mouth was kissing her ear.

"How could there be if I'm really Duncan Ely? I mean, that makes Roxanne my daughter."

"Seriously."

"There's nothing going on. Seriously. I told you that."

She put her arms around his neck and kissed him.

Now she was happy again.

Her imaginings now seemed lurid and foolish, and she wondered how she could have let herself become so childish as to believe, even momentarily, in the supernatural. Yes, Myles was different. He was changing his whole life —who wouldn't be different? Oddly, she didn't mind the change. Switching back to the piano was an enormous gamble, but somehow she felt it was a gamble he was going to win. When she came home from the Beach Bum at night, she would hear him practicing on the Steinway. He was so good she couldn't believe that he wouldn't bowl over the critics. She still didn't understand how he had become so good, but the fact remained he was. He was full of enthusiasm and drive. He was happier than she'd ever seen him. If the piano was what he really wanted, then she didn't care if he gave up his writing. Ultimately, all she wanted was his happiness and his love.

Perhaps, she thought, perhaps Duncan Ely was the best thing that ever happened to us.

He was now driving himself eight and ten hours a day, preparing for the debut. Scales, fantastically difficult finger exercises, pounding octaves; polishing the difficult program he was going to play. He had a drive for perfection that fascinated her. He had even bought an electronic pitch-finder and a tuning wrench so that every morning he would tune the piano to perfect pitch. "Does it need it every *day?*" she asked, wonderingly.

"I bang it so hard, it goes out a little. Not much, but a little. I like to keep it right on pitch."

One night he practiced till two in the morning. The music, rolling out of the skylight, elicited howls from the neighbors and a visit from the police. Myles was apologetic and promised he would stop playing at ten. The cop left, and Paula commented dryly, "The neighbors must really love us."

"They shouldn't complain," said Myles. "They're getting a Carnegie Hall performance free."

They went to bed, and Myles made love to her. She wondered where his inexhaustible energy came from.

The multifaceted Maggie was handling not only the redecoration and stocking of Beach Bum North but public relations for its opening as well. They didn't have the money to take more than a small ad in the *Times*, so she was relying on word of mouth and Roxanne to publicize the new store. When she told Paula she was going to ask Roxanne to help her draw up the invitation list for the opening, Paula's reaction was negative.

"Why not?" asked Maggie. "She's already helped us. Why wouldn't she help us again?"

"I just don't want to ask her," said Paula.

"Darling, just because you're jealous of her—"

"That's not true."

"Don't fool Maggie."

"It's not! It's just that she's helping Myles, and I hate to impose."

"All she can say is no. And remember, babe, we've got four thou each riding on the success of this place. Roxanne can make it for us if she gets her social register buddies to come to the opening. So whether you like it or not, I'm going to ask her."

She did. And Roxanne agreed. She did more than help Maggie make up the list. She got on the phone and called many of the people receiving invitations, praising the new store to the skies and urging them to come. Maggie was ecstatic.

The day of the opening was fortunately clear and warm.

The doors opened at noon, and the Swirling Purples, the rock combo Maggie had hired, began playing at one. Free soft drinks were being given out, and after four, free cocktails and canapes. For the first few hours there was a trickle of customers and Maggie was chewing her nails. But at three things began to pick up. And by five, when Paula arrived from the downtown store, the place was jammed.

The store's decoration was wild. The Personality Posters of Humphrey Bogart, Theda Bara, Peter Fonda on his motorcycle, the Maharishi, Ravi Shankar, Ringo Starr, Marlon Brando and Shirley Temple studded the walls and ceiling, enframed in the kaleidoscopic psychedelic murals Jimmy Ress had painted. Tiny white bulbs had been strung around each poster, and they blinked like miniature marquees, lending an even more turned-on quality to the electric ambience. The Swirling Purples were squeezed into the center island between bathing suits and beach robes, from where their electronic amplifiers twanged and thumped a steady flow of New Sound music. Tall skinny models in bathing suits squeezed through the well-dressed crowd with white-jacketed waiters following in their wake holding trays of drinks and hors d'oeuvres.

"It's a smash!" screamed Maggie over the deafening noise as she hugged Paula and Myles. "They're loving it! And *everybody* came!"

In fact Roxanne's phone calls had turned out a very fashionable crowd. The Jet Set, the *Social Register* Set, and the Theater Set were all well represented, and Suzy was there taking it all down. Even Lauren Bacall made a brief appearance, which sent Maggie and Paula into orbit.

Paula hadn't spoken to Roxanne since she had learned of Myles' career switch. She had purposely avoided talking to her, partially because she was ashamed of spying on her and partially because she still resented her influence on Myles, even though she was convinced their relationship was Platonic.

Now there was no avoiding her.

She pushed her way through the crowd to where Roxanne, dressed in a white crocheted mini-cocktail dress, was talking with Princess Ina Andrassy. Spotting Paula, she turned and smiled.

"Your store is simply marvelous!" she said. "Congratulations."

"It was all Maggie's doing, not me. And I wanted to thank you for helping to get such a great turnout."

"I was glad to help. Besides, it wasn't difficult. Everyone was dying to see the place. I have only one complaint."

"What's that?"

"That *band!*" She made a face and pointed to the Swirling Purples, who were twanging their way through a particularly loud number. "They're driving me deaf!"

Paula smiled.

"I'm afraid we're stuck with them, at least today."

"That's why I can't stand discotheques: they're so incredibly loud. The music I rather like. But the volume! But tell me: Aren't you excited about Myles?"

Paula took a Scotch from a passing waiter.

"Well, it came as sort of a shock."

"Oh, I know. And I'm afraid we were a little devious about it." (*Devious?* thought Paula. It was like a spy ring!) "But Myles thought it was so important to make sure before he told you. I can understand why, can't you?"

"Oh, yes. I know he thought I'd be upset about taking such a gamble. But he wants to try it, and that's the important thing as far as I'm concerned."

Roxanne squeezed her arm.

"You're a marvelous wife for him. Most women think of nothing but security—their own security, which they think is more important than their husband's happiness. Myles' happiness is the piano, and he's going to have a brilliant career. My father spotted his talent, and I must say his judgment is being borne out. I think Myles is brilliant, don't you?"

"Brilliant's hardly the word for it. I still can't believe the change in his playing. I'm not expert by any means, but even I can tell he's good. More than good: great. I have no idea how he's done it."

"Philip Rosen is terribly excited about him. He's making all the arrangements for the debut, and he'll make sure all the important critics are there, as well as the important record people. Don't be surprised if Myles becomes the hot young pianist before long. Take my word for it, he's going to have a career as brilliant as my father's."

There doesn't seem to be a trace of envy in the woman, thought Paula. Shouldn't there be? Shouldn't a woman as devoted to her father as she was be a little jealous of a young man who might put her father's reputation in the shade?

But she obviously isn't. If anything, she seems happy as a lark about the whole thing. Of course, if Myles *is* Duncan, she wouldn't be jealous. . . .

Stop it, Paula, she thought. Stop it right now.

Myles is Myles.

The opening was to continue till ten.

At nine thirty the crowd was still as packed as ever and no one looked ready to leave. While Maggie was delighted at the success of the party, she began to worry. Squeezing up to Myles, she said, "Some of them are beginning to get smashed. Do you think I should close the bar?"

"The invitations said drinks till ten, didn't they?"

"Yes, but I didn't think they'd stay this long."

"You only have a half hour more, so don't panic. No one will break up the place, and if you stop the drinks now, people will call you a chintz."

She sighed.

"I suppose you're right. So, what do you think of the place?"

"I like it. You've done a great job. I'm sorry Paula couldn't be more of a help."

"Don't be silly. One of us had to run the downtown store. I couldn't have done anything without her."

"I suppose." He frowned and stared down at the floor thoughtfully. "Maggie," he said after a moment, "have you noticed anything strange about Paula?"

"Strange?" She looked surprised. "No. Why?"

"I'm worried about her."

"Because of Roxanne?"

"Why Roxanne?"

"Paula's jealous of her. But I don't call that strange. If I were your wife, I'd be jealous of Roxanne too."

He smiled.

"No, I wasn't thinking of that. I know she's jealous, but she knows she doesn't have anything to be jealous of as far as Roxanne and I are concerned. What I was thinking of was her mind."

"What's wrong with her mind?"

"Well, she's gotten a strange sort of obsession lately. And please—not a word of this to her. You understand."

"Of course not. But what obsession? She looks completely unobsessed to me. Of course, I'm not sure how obsessed people are supposed to look—"

"It's pretty weird. She thinks I'm someone else. In fact, she thinks I'm Duncan Ely."

Now Maggie looked truly surprised.

"Duncan Ely? Myles, darling, you sort of lost me a while back—"

"She thinks I'm a reincarnation of Duncan Ely. That when he died, his soul went into my body. That my mind, or my personality or whatever you're going to call it, is really Duncan Ely's."

"Good God, that's wild!"

"No kidding. She asked me point blank the other night if I was Duncan Ely. I knew something was bothering her—she seemed almost afraid of me. But I had no idea what it was until she came right out and said it."

"What did you tell her?"

"I told her I wasn't, of course. What was I going to say: Yes, I am Duncan Ely. How did you guess?"

"Then what happened?"

He shrugged.

"She got all excited and relieved and started hugging and kissing me."

"Apparently she believed you. So at least she doesn't think you're Duncan Ely any longer. That's something."

"But, Maggie, the fact that she could think such a crazy thing at *all*! My God. . . ." He hesitated. "Look, she seems to be all right now, so maybe whatever it was has gone now. But if it happens again, what do you think I should do?"

Maggie frowned.

"I don't know. Talk to Chuck, I suppose. He'd know better than I."

"And if she says anything to you about my being Duncan's reincarnation, you'll tell me?"

"Oh, sure, except I don't *expect* her to. She may be going crackers on the sly, but she certainly looks normal to me. Unless. . . . You don't suppose she might be taking drugs, do you?"

"I don't know what to think. All I know is, I hope to God nothing's really wrong with her mind. Nothing permanent."

"I hope so too. But I doubt it. As I said, she looks perfectly normal to me. Or as normal as the rest of us, which may not be saying much."

Myles looked past Maggie.

"Here she comes. Remember, not a word to her."

"I know. Not a word."

The opening party had cost Maggie and Paula twelve hundred dollars which, with the cost of buying stock and redecorating, wiped out all but a few hundred of the eight thousand they had borrowed. But the money was well spent, because the papers gave the shop good notices. By the end of their first week, the store had become an exciting new in place and was making money.

Paula continued to run the downtown store alone, although Maggie had hired two salesgirls to help her uptown. The original store was prospering also, and Paula realized with mounting excitement that she and Maggie could possibly pay off the bank loan a year sooner than they expected. Once it was paid, they might clear as much as fifteen thousand a year each off the two stores.

One day two weeks before Myles' debut, he called her at the shop and told her Abby had come home from school early.

"Is anything wrong?" asked Paula, anxiously.

"She has a cough and a runny nose. The teacher thought she might be catching the flu, so she sent her home. I put her in bed and called Chuck. He's going to come by on his way home and have a look at her."

"It's nothing serious, is it?"

"Oh, no. She feels all right. Don't worry. I'll keep an eye on her."

"I can close up and come home, if you think I should."

"No—really. She's fine."

She hung up, deciding she'd close early anyway.

*

She got home at five thirty to find Chuck coming out of Abby's bedroom.

"Is it the flu?" she asked. He nodded. "A mild case. She has about half a degree of fever. But there's really nothing to worry about."

"But she had flu shots—"

Chuck shrugged.

"What can I tell you? Sometimes they don't work."

He left some pills which Abby was supposed to take three times a day. Then he went upstairs and had a quick drink before he went home.

Myles seemed edgy. After Chuck had gone, Paula asked him if something was bothering him.

"Oh, no. I guess maybe I'm getting nervous about the debut, that's all."

She made some hot soup and sandwiches and took them down to Abby, who seemed not at all bothered by her flu. In fact, she was delighted she was getting out of school for a few days.

She asked if she could watch television. Paula said yes and turned on the set, tuning in to *Star Trek*. Abby became instantly absorbed in the problems of the twenty-third century.

Robin curled up on the floor beside her bed and went to sleep.

The next night when Paula came home, Abby's sore throat was almost gone, and with it the cough and the runny nose.

Paula sat down on her bed and smiled.

"You look awfully healthy to me, young lady."

"I feel fine except for my foot," replied Abby.

"What's wrong with your foot?"

"Oh—" She stared at the ceiling. "Well, it aches."

"Uh-huh. In other words, you're dreaming up something new so you won't have to go back to school."

Abby grinned sheepishly.

"Well, it *did* ache a little. Do I really have to go back to school?"

"I'm afraid so. Did you take a nice long nap this afternoon?"

"Yes, until the man woke me up."

"What man?"

"The man in the funny black hat."

Her attention returned to the old movie she was watching, *The Loves of Andy Hardy*. Paula frowned.

"What man in what funny black hat?"

"He was upstairs talking to Daddy. I don't know who he was. But I heard them arguing and that's what woke me up. Who's the actor that plays Andy Hardy?"

"Mickey Rooney."

"Who's he? I never heard of him."

"He's an actor," said Paula, impatiently. "Did you see this man?"

"Uh-huh. I went halfway up the stairs and looked in the gold mirror on the landing, so I could watch them but they couldn't see me. He was sitting in a chair, and Daddy was standing in front of him. Daddy looked scared."

"Scared? Why?"

"I don't know. Does Mickey Rooney still make movies?"

"Every once in a while. What did the man in the black hat look like?"

"Oh, he was young and nice-looking. Except he looked sort of—well, mad."

"What were they arguing about?"

"I didn't hear it all. But the man said, 'You've got to do it *now*,' and then Daddy said something like he didn't want to do it or something, and the man said he *had* to do it because it was part of the contract. And don't ask me what he had to do, because I came back down and got back in bed. I like Mickey Rooney. I wish he'd make a new movie."

Paula kissed her and got up.

She found Myles upstairs sitting at the piano looking over the score of the "Hammerklavier Sonata," which he had decided to play in the debut.

"Darling, who was here this afternoon?" she asked.

"No one. Why?"

"Abby said there was a man here who was arguing with you. A man with a black hat."

She could have sworn Myles looked momentarily terrified. His face turned chalk white, although he kept his eyes glued to the score to avoid having to look at her.

"Oh, yes, that was Bill Grainger. He's one of Philip Rosen's publicity boys. He dropped by to talk about a tour Philip's trying to line up for me."

"A tour? When?"

"I don't know yet. It can't be set till after the reviews come out. If the reviews are bad, there won't be a tour."

"But Abby said you two were arguing."

"She must have been mistaken."

"She said he wanted you to do something right away. Something you didn't want to do."

"Oh, that." Myles looked up and smiled. "He wants me to go on the *Merv Griffin Show*. I told him it was a mistake to do it before the debut. I mean, who knows who I am now? Maybe later, but not now."

She sat down and leafed through the new *Time* which had arrived that morning. After a moment, she said, "Does this Bill what's-his-name always leave his hat on in the house?"

"What?"

"His hat. Does he always leave it on in the house?"

Silence for a moment.

"I guess he does. Don't ask me why. I've only met him a couple of times. I want to run through the fugue in the 'Hammerklavier' a few times before dinner. Okay?"

"Go ahead."

During dinner, Paula asked, "Was Bill Grainger a friend of Duncan Ely's?"

Myles trimmed the fat off his lamb chop.

"They probably knew each other. I don't know if they were friends."

"I think I saw him at Duncan's funeral. Just as we were leaving the cemetery, I saw a man in a black Derby hat step up to the grave and pour some oil on the coffin—just like Roxanne had done."

"Really? I didn't notice him at the funeral."

"Myles, do you suppose Satanism wasn't just a joke with Duncan? That he believed it and practiced it in secret? And that the rest of them—Roxanne, Philip, this Grainger person—they were all part of it too?"

"What makes you ask that?"

"For one thing, the weird things they did at his funeral."

Myles chewed his lamb chop and gave her a sarcastic look.

"You're probably right. I'll bet they all dance around toadstools by the light of the moon and fly broomsticks and have a high old time."

Paula, irritated by his flippancy, dropped the subject.

That night, something came in the house. Something menacing. Except it wasn't her house. It was a dream house, an Andrew Wyeth house, a huge ruined nineteenth-century house with holes in the roof and weeds growing through the floors. The window panes were shattered, and a soft breeze blew through them, billowing the ragged lace curtains. Outside the house was a forest of gnarled cypress trees; their branches scratched across the roof as the breeze bent them.

Paula had never seen the house, and she couldn't understand why she was there, even in her dreams. She was standing on the landing of the rickety wooden stairway whose railing had fallen off. The stairs led down to the huge living room with the billowing lace curtains. There was no furniture except a brass bed in the center of the room.

Something was in the house.

She turned and looked at the huge cracked mirror on the wall of the landing. Like her own mirror, it reflected the upstairs above her.

The man in the black Derby hat was looking down at her.

"You have to do it," he said. "You have to do it *now*."

"Do what?" she cried.

"You know. It must be done now."

"What am I supposed to *do?*"

The man looked at her coldly.

"I'm not talking to you."

A chill wind rushed through the house and up the stairs. Paula shivered and looked down. Duncan Ely was climbing the stairs toward her. She pressed back against the mirror, transfixed by the sight of the mouldering corpse. The dark blue suit he had been buried in was eaten away in several places; his skin had taken on a greenish-black color. His eyes were open, but he didn't seem to see her, for as he reached the landing he passed by her without looking at her. Then he climbed to the second floor.

"I'm ready to do it," he said to the man in the black Derby hat.

"Good."

They went into a room, leaving the door open. She heard Mickey Rooney inside the room. He was arguing with Judge Hardy over whether he could have the judge's car to take Ann Rutherford—or was it Gloria Jean?—to the high school prom.

She ran up the stairs.

"Stay away from her!" she screamed. "Stay away from Abby!"

She was halfway to the second floor when her legs became heavy and she started running in the slow motion of dreams. Each stair seemed to take hours to climb. Duncan

Ely appeared in the door of the room. He was holding the small porcelain phial, the one with the howling Gorgons on its sides. Now he seemed to see her.

"I'm sorry," he said. "I don't want to do it. She's a nice little girl. But you see, I have no choice. It has to be done now."

"Don't! Please don't—" cried Paula.

"I'm sorry."

He returned to the room. She looked back at the mirror. It had grown larger now, so that it filled the entire stairwell and reflected the inside of the room. Abby was asleep on a bed. On the far side of the bed stood Mickey Rooney arguing with Lewis Stone over possession of the Hardy family car. On the near side stood Duncan Ely and the man in the black Derby hat. Duncan held the phial over Abby's face. From somewhere downstairs someone began to play the "Mephisto Waltz."

"Don't!" screamed Paula.

He tilted the phial and poured some oil on Abby's forehead.

The wind blew through the house, rattling the window frames and drowning out the music. Abby was saying, "Mommy, Mommy, Mommy—"

Paula felt a hand on her shoulder. She woke up.

"Mommy," said Abby, who was standing by the bed. "Mommy, I don't feel good."

Now Paula was awake. She sat up and turned on the light. Myles was beside her, asleep. She took Abby's hand.

"What's wrong, darling?"

"I don't feel good. My throat tickles, and I feel hot and then I feel cold."

Paula put her hand on her forehead. It was hot. Was she imagining it, or did it also feel slightly slick? As if oil had been poured on it, then dabbed off. . . .

She woke her husband. "Myles, call Chuck. Abby's got a fever." It was four thirty in the morning. Paula took Abby back to her room and tucked her in bed. Then she got the thermometer from the bathroom, shook it down and took her temperature.

Myles came into the room.

"Chuck says to give her two more of the pills, and he'll come around first thing in the morning."

"Tell him to come *now!*" snapped Paula. "She's got a hundred and two temperature!"

Myles looked frightened. He hurried back into their room. She heard him talking to Chuck. When he arrived, twenty minutes later, looking sleepy and irritable, she gave him a mug of the coffee she had made, then he went into Abby's room. When he came out, he said, "Don't ask me how she got it, but it looks like she's caught pneumonia."

"Oh, my God," said Paula.

"I gave her a shot of penicillin, which ought to stop it. I'll come back on my way to the hospital and take another look at her."

"She'll be all right, won't she?" said Paula, anxiously.

"Oh sure. There's nothing to worry about, although she is running a high fever. If that gets worse, we may have to put her in the hospital for a couple of days. But she'll get over it."

When he returned four hours later, her temperature had gone up another degree and a half. Paula was frantic.

"Should we put her in the hospital?" she said.

Chuck nodded.

"I'll send an ambulance down and arrange a room for her."

"But isn't the penicillin working?" asked Myles.

"It hasn't seemed to do much good yet. I'll give her some more when we get her moved. Will one of you come in the ambulance with her?"

"We both will," said Myles.

"Okay. Get her things packed. I'll see you at the hospital. And look, you two: don't worry."

" 'Don't worry,' he says!" said Paula.

He held up his hand.

"I know. But don't. We can handle it. It's just that sometimes it takes the penicillin a while to show any effects."

They spent the day at St. Vincent's, leafing through back issues of *Life*, *Cosmopolitan* and *True*, drinking endless cups of bad coffee, eating Drake's Cakes and waiting.

At eleven o'clock, Chuck came into the waiting room. His face didn't look encouraging.

"We've put her on heavy antibiotics," he said, "and we've got her under an ice blanket."

"An ice blanket? Why?"

"To try and get the fever down. It's a hundred and four point five."

She started to cry. Myles put his arm around her.

"Paulie, she'll be okay—"

"But I don't understand! It's all happening so *fast*—"

"I know," said Chuck. "It's unusual. There's something complicating the pneumonia, but until we finish the tests on her we can't be sure what it is."

"But can't you do *something?*"

Chuck squeezed her shoulder.

"Of course, as soon as we finish the tests, which shouldn't be more than an hour. Then we'll get her fixed up."

She nodded slowly, trying to stop the hysteria she felt.

"You'll let us know as soon as there's any change?"

"We'll let you know the moment the fever breaks."

*

She died at five o'clock that afternoon.

The fever had reached a hundred and six at two thirty. Chuck reported she was delirious. He warned Paula and Myles of the possibility of brain damage if the fever didn't subside.

At ten after five, he came out and told them. He looked numb.

"I don't know what to say," he told them. "I feel so damned helpless—"

Paula was trying to realize what had happened.

"It wasn't your fault, Chuck. You tried—"

She turned to Myles. Her face was twisted with grief. She started to sob.

"Oh, Abby. . . . My darling Abby. . . ."

They took her into Chuck's office, where he gave her a sedative. She was hysterical.

"The *oil* did it," she sobbed.

"The what?" asked Chuck.

"The oil. The oil Duncan Ely poured on her forehead. I felt it on her skin when she came in this morning. It wasn't just a dream. He poured oil on her forehead and it *killed* her!"

Chuck looked blankly at Myles. He shook his head.

"The oil! It's something horrible and evil—like Duncan Ely and that man in the hat. . . ."

She turned around and glared at Myles. Tears were streaming down her face.

"Who *is* he, Myles?"

"Who is who?"

"That man in the black Derby hat! He's not Bill Grainger—I know it! He killed Abby, and you know who he is! Now *tell* me!"

Myles looked shocked.

"Paula, please—"

"Tell me!" she screamed. "Tell me who he is!"

"He's Bill Grainger—"

"He's not! I know he's not! Tell me, Myles! Tell me! *You* know!"

Chuck shook her roughly.

"Paula, calm down. You're going to make yourself sick. Calm down."

She sank into a chair and buried her face in her hands.

"Oh, God," she said, "what's happening to me? And what happened to Abby?"

The fantasy had become reality.

Part III

1

For the next two days she was numb.

She stayed in Abby's bedroom, slowly going through her clothes and toys, separating and packing them away, automatically falling back on motherly habit as a narcotic to dull the shock of her daughter's sudden death. Periodically she would try to cry, but she couldn't. There were no tears left, just a numbing pain.

Myles tried to comfort her, but she asked him to let her alone. Her outburst in the hospital had been unpreventable. Afterward, she had weakly apologized to both Chuck and Myles, for as she had become rational again she realized her accusations had been unjust. Myles was apparently as heartbroken as she was over Abby's death, and it was unfair of her to throw her dreams and fantasies up in his face at such a horrible moment—to accuse him of some sort of complicity in his own daughter's death—when she hadn't a shred of factual evidence to back up her imaginings. For this she felt ashamed. Still, she couldn't rid herself of the feeling that what she had blurted out so hysterically was closer to the truth than Chuck's conviction that Abby had become infected by a virulent form of pneumococcal meningitis.

The result was an agonizing ambivalence toward her husband: an unhappy mixture of love for the old Myles and fear and suspicion of what she thought of as the new one. This, on top of her grief, left her in a mood of utter depression; the one time in her life she desperately needed someone to hang on to, that someone had become an unknown quantity, a flickering shadow, one moment familiar, the next a complete stranger. Consequently, she drew into herself; and her relationship with Myles became a frosty void.

Somehow she managed to get through the funeral.

Janet, who had flown up from Fort Lauderdale, looked ten years older from the shock and was so depressed that Myles had to spend a good deal of his time in her hotel room to keep her from breaking down completely. Maggie volunteered to do anything she could to be of assistance, which Paula appreciated, though in her distraction there was nothing she could think of to ask her to do. To her surprise, Roxanne arrived at the apartment the morning of the funeral with a large casserole she had baked, explaining that bringing food was a New England custom and that she remembered how grateful she had been when some of her New England friends had brought food when her child died.

"I didn't know you'd had children," Paula said.

"I had a son. He was badly retarded, and he only lived six weeks. Now I think it was probably a blessing that he died. But then—it didn't seem like a blessing then."

For the first time, Paula felt a twinge of sympathy for the coldly beautiful woman.

"I'm sorry," she said, simply.

To her relief, Roxanne offered to take Robin back and try and find a new home for him. When she left with the black Labrador, Paula felt the dog was the one thing that had belonged to Abby that she wasn't reluctant to part with.

After the funeral, the tears came in a flood.

They drove her home in the long black limousine. Maggie offered to prepare a lunch, but Paula begged off, slipped out of the house and went to a movie. It was an odd place to go, but she had to get away from the house and from Myles. She wanted to be alone; somehow she had to purge herself of her misery. So she went to Loew's Sheridan and sat through a Doris Day comedy and a Henry Fonda Western. The theater was practically empty, for which she was thankful. She sat in a back row and cried, staring at the images on the screen but completely oblivious to what they were doing and saying. She thought of Abby, only a few days before so alive and happy, and now sealed in a box in the ground. Her stomach felt knives of pain as she quietly sobbed.

It was an unusual therapy, but it worked, to a degree. When she came out of the theater, her eyes were red but she had stopped crying. The pain was beginning to die slowly. She knew she would survive. She would pick up the routine of her life and stumble back to some semblance of normality. It would be difficult, but what else could she do? Abby was gone forever. No one returned from the grave—or did they? She remembered the odd smile on Myles' face that time in Bermuda when he had made some inane remark about only living once.

Had Duncan Ely managed to live twice?

That night, Myles asked her if she thought he should cancel his debut.

"Of course not. Why should you?"

"I thought because of Abby—"

"Not playing at Carnegie Hall isn't going to bring her back."

She knew she was being cold to him, but she couldn't help herself. He took offense.

"Paula, do you still believe those things you said in the hospital?"

She found her old TarGard and inserted a new Viceroy in it. The urge to smoke had never left her, and in her present state of mind she didn't have the strength to fight it any longer. She inhaled deeply, blowing the smoke out through her nostrils.

"I told you I was sorry about that."

"I know. But you've been acting so chilly—"

"If I have, I haven't meant to be."

"But I really don't know what you were talking about! 'Oil'—what oil? How can oil kill anyone? And I told you the man was Bill Grainger. Ask Phil Rosen—he'll tell you."

"I said I believe you."

They looked at each other like two boxers slowly circling the ring, each waiting for the other to lower his guard.

She wanted to reach out to him, to reestablish contact; but she couldn't, because she didn't trust him.

She kept her guard up.

*

"Paula, dear, what's happened with you and Myles?" asked Janet as they sat in Kennedy waiting for her plane to Fort Lauderdale. Myles had gone to check her tickets.

"Nothing's happened that I know of," said Paula, dully lighting another cigarette. After taking up the habit again, she found herself smoking more than she ever had before.

"He tells me you suspect him of, well, of having something to do with Abby's sickness."

"I've told him I don't think that. If he doesn't believe me, it's not my fault."

"But, darling, you two have hardly spoken to each other since I've been here! You used to be so happy together— and I know Myles is upset about it."

"How do you know?"

"He told me. Besides, I know my son. I can tell when he's upset."

The numbness suddenly left Paula's mind. Of course, she would know! She's his mother, his own flesh and blood! She would know. . . .

She looked toward the reservation desk. Myles was still standing in line with Janet's ticket. She turned back to her mother-in-law.

"Janet, have you noticed anything different about Myles?"

"Different? I told you he's upset about how you're treating him—"

"No, I mean different in his habits. In his . . . his personality. Does he seem to have *changed* somehow?"

Janet blinked.

"Well, yes."

"How?"

"He's going to be a pianist again. Personally, I always thought he should have stuck with the piano. Just because he got a few bad reviews—"

"I don't mean that. Does he seem like a different person somehow? Like someone *else?*"

"Darling, I don't know what you're talking about—"

Paula sighed.

"No, I suppose you don't. I'm not even sure *I* know what I'm talking about at this point."

Janet looked at her curiously.

"You're just upset, which is only natural. You know, it might do you good to see a doctor. I mean, a psychiatrist. They can do wonders for you when you're depressed. I know that when my second husband died, I felt like the world was coming to an end. But a few sessions with Dr. Arnheim, and I was feeling like a new woman again. Would you like me to give you his address? He's still at the same place on Central Park West."

Paula shook her head.

"No, thanks. I don't need a psychiatrist. At least not yet."

She ground out her cigarette and watched as Myles crossed the waiting room toward them.

"We've got fifteen minutes before you board," he said. "Did you take your tranquilizers?"

Janet nodded.

"And fifteen minutes gives me nice time for a stiff Scotch to *really* knock me out."

They headed for the bar.

Now her life seemed empty.

She went back to the Beach Bum, trying to fill her time with the mechanics of work, but she really wasn't interested in selling bathing suits. She was haunted by the ghost of her daughter and the strange man in the black Derby hat. She couldn't rid herself of the conviction that somehow what she had dreamed was the truth, that what had actually happened that night had filtered through her sleeping mind and distorted itself into the language of dreams. But how could she prove it? She tried to force her mind to recreate the dream by concentrating on the strange ruined house before she went to sleep. She remembered it clearly: the gaping holes in the roof, the ragged lace curtains over the shattered windows, the brass bed standing in the middle of the immense room. But, perversely, the more she tried to dream, the more dreamless her sleep became.

Then she had an idea. She pulled out a copy of the *Times* Sunday magazine and reread the article Myles had written about Duncan Ely. Roxanne's husband, William de Lancre. Perhaps the reason for their divorce was the retarded child Roxanne had told her about. But perhaps it was something else—something that would open a window to Paula. She decided she would try to see him.

She called the brokerage firm of De Lancre, Reardon and Lord and asked to speak to him. When he came on the phone, she told him she was a friend of his ex-wife and wanted to talk to him about "a personal matter." For a moment he didn't say anything. She wondered if he might think she wanted something out of him—perhaps money. Whatever he thought, he was scrupulously polite. He asked her if two o'clock the next afternoon would be convenient. She agreed.

The offices of De Lancre, Reardon and Lord were on Pine Street, a half block from Wall Street, on the sixth, seventh and eighth floors of an older office building whose dingy turn-of-the-century facade gave an impression of solidity and integrity that the new chrome-and-glass buildings in the financial district could never duplicate. Paula nervously smoked a cigarette in the reception room until a middle-aged secretary appeared and led her down a corridor to a large paneled office furnished with worn leather chairs and huge sailing prints on the walls. William de Lancre met her at the door, smiled and shook her hand. He was in his early forties, though he could easily have passed for a man ten years younger. He was even more handsome than he had looked in the photograph in Myles' article, having dark curly hair and a square face with eyes as blue as Paul Newman's. He was dressed in a conservative Brooks Brothers suit and had a friendly, almost courtly, manner that seemed old-fashioned but quite in keeping with the Harvard accent and New York Yacht Club tie. As he led her to an overstuffed leather chair in front of his desk, Paula noticed a number of issues of *Yachting* magazine interspersed with the *Wall Street Journals* spread around the room.

"Your name seems familiar to me," he said after he sat down behind his desk. "Didn't you write that article on Duncan Ely that was in the *Times* last month?"

"My husband wrote it."

"It was very well done, I thought. Duncan was quite an extraordinary man. Did you ever meet him?"

"Yes. About two months before he died, when my husband went to interview him for the article."

For a moment, neither said anything. He was obviously waiting for her to tell him what she wanted. She was desperately trying to think of the best way to open the "personal matter."

"Mr. de Lancre," she finally said, "in a way I feel terribly foolish coming to you. In fact, I'm not quite sure what I want to ask you. But last week, my daughter died—"

"I'm sorry," he interrupted, sympathetically.

"She got sick quite suddenly, and was dead within twenty-four hours. The doctors aren't really sure what it was that killed her. But—" My God, she thought, how *can* I say this? "But I have a feeling that somehow my husband and your ex-wife are involved in it."

Now the friendly, courtly, New York Yacht Club manner was replaced by amazement.

"Excuse me, Mrs. Clarkson, but I'm not quite following you. Involved in what way?"

She gestured helplessly.

"I'm not *sure!* That's why I had to see you. I thought maybe you could tell me something—I don't know what—" Stop it, she thought. You're getting excited; you're going to cry and make a fool of yourself. Be calm. Be rational. Don't let him think you're a silly, neurotic woman. Tell him everything slowly and clearly.

She did. She told him about meeting Duncan, about the change in Myles after Duncan died, about the miraculous improvement in his playing and his decision to try a concert career.

"A concert career? Like Duncan's?"

"Exactly like Duncan's. My husband had started out to

be a pianist but hadn't done well. Duncan encouraged him to take it up again. He even left him fifty thousand dollars in his will to help him do it. Now Roxanne and Philip Rosen have arranged for him to give a debut in Carnegie Hall next Saturday night, and I think probably he's going to be very successful."

She hesitated. He was trying to be courteous, but she could tell he was confused by what she was saying.

"I don't quite see what this has to do with your daughter," he said. "Or me."

She squeezed her fists, trying to fight her nervousness.

"While you were married to Roxanne, did you ever meet a young man who wears a black Derby hat?"

Was she imagining it, or was there a spark of recognition in his blue eyes? His face remained immobile, but wasn't there something in his eyes? Or was it that she merely hoped there would be something?

"I'm afraid not. Why do you ask?"

"Because this man, whoever he is, this man is somehow connected with my husband and Roxanne, and—" Oh, God, he thinks I'm insane! He must! "Was there ever anything about Roxanne that struck you as odd? Something about her that seemed hidden, or—or devious?"

Now the blue eyes became wary and the handsome face almost hostile.

"I'm sorry, Mrs. Clarkson, but I don't believe I can be of any assistance to you."

"I know I have no right to ask you these things, but I have to know! There must have been something you noticed—"

He stood up.

"I don't think it will do either of us any good to continue this."

She blurted out, "Were Roxanne and Duncan Satanists?"

He stared at her a moment, then flipped a switch on his intercom.

"Mrs. Daley, Mrs. Clarkson is ready to leave now."

"Yes, Mr. de Lancre."

Paula got to her feet. She felt asinine.

"I'm sorry," she said. "I know what you must think, but I had to ask."

He said nothing. Trying to look as composed as possible, she crossed the room to the door. The secretary opened it. Paula turned and looked back at the desk.

"Thank you for your time," she said, quietly.

Then she left the room.

When she came out of the building onto Pine Street, the narrow sidewalks were thronged with clerks, stockbrokers, mutual fund executives and tellers all pushing and hurrying their way back to their cubicles from lunch. She bumped her way along with the crowd, feeling embarrassed to the point of wanting to hide. How could I have done it? she thought. I'm a lady—God knows, I *think* I am—and to barge into that office and ask a complete stranger if his ex-wife is a Satanist! How could I?

A man in a black Derby hat bumped into her. She twirled around, horrified.

The man was an elderly banker with a white carnation in his buttonhole.

"I'm sorry," he mumbled and hurried on.

Feeling like screaming, she started to run toward the subway station.

She no longer saw much of Myles.

When she came home from the Beach Bum, he would be upstairs practicing. She would look in on him, say hello, then go into the kitchen and cook dinner. Sometimes they would eat together; more often, he would continue practicing until she had finished her meal. Then, when she had gone downstairs, he would eat alone and return to his piano. She would lie on her bed, staring at the ceiling or trying to read *The Confessions of Nat Turner*, while from the room above her the piano thundered and sang, preventing her any peace and causing her to come to hate music. At ten he would stop and she would pretend to go to sleep so she wouldn't have to talk to him. Sometimes he would "wake" her up to make love to her. She would submit uncomplainingly, but there was no longer any tenderness to it. It was cold, a mere satisfaction of an itch. The fact that the itch was still there shamed her, for she had always associated the physical Myles with his personality, assuming her sexual desire for him was merely a facet of her love for him. Now she was embarrassed to find she still hungered for the physical Myles even though she suspected the personality she had loved had either changed beyond recognition, or was dead.

She took no interest in his piano career. That had died
with Abby. She was vaguely aware that the debut was only
a few days away. She knew that Philip Rosen called at
least once every night to check on his new client. Roxanne
telephoned frequently too, polite as always to Paula but
obviously impatient to talk to Myles. Paula would give
him the phone and go back to bed, wondering why her
jealousy of Roxanne had dulled to a mere ache. Perhaps
she was growing used to the situation.

Perhaps—even worse—she no longer cared.

Carnegie Hall was not filled for Myles' debut, but it was
surprisingly well attended for a performance of an unknown pianist, and the crowd, thanks to Roxanne, was a
fashionable one. Even the weather seemed propitious: it
was a balmy spring evening. As Paula stepped out of the
cab in front of the beautifully renovated old building, she
wished she could feel some emotion, some sense of excitement, about an evening that would normally have been
one of the most important nights of her life. But she felt
nothing.

She went backstage to Myles' dressing room, which was
filled with flowers, including the roses she had sent. Roxanne was there, looking stunning in a pale yellow Mainbocher gown, and as she kissed Paula she complimented
her on her white Ohrbach's dress, pretending she had
never seen it before. Paula played the game, pretending
she was glad to see Roxanne; then she kissed Myles. He
looked surprisingly calm. He was in a new set of tails and
looked handsome—more handsome than she'd ever seen

him. He has a sense of style to him, she thought. A self-confidence that he never had before—or is it arrogance?

"You don't look nervous," she said, at a loss to think of anything more personal to say to a man who had become almost a total stranger.

"I am, though. My palms are sweating. But I haven't got as bad a case of the shakes as I thought I would."

"Everyone is nervous before a performance," said Roxanne. "Even my father was. The nervousness gives the performance its excitement."

Philip Rosen had come in. "Myles is going to be stupendous," he said. "He'll knock them dead."

"Everyone important came," added Roxanne. "They'll spread the word. By tomorrow morning New York will know something exciting has happened."

Paula had the feeling the three of them were waiting for her to go, so she wished Myles good luck, left the room and made her way to her seat in the fifth row of the orchestra. The elegant white auditorium with its deep red seats was brightly lighted, and on the stage the huge black concert grand stood silently waiting, as it had thousands of times before, to crucify or glorify the hopeful who would soon come out to play it. Paula saw Harold Schonberg of the *Times.* She saw Sydney Raymont with Dame Agatha Renfrew sitting next to him, looking like an aging sybil. Four rows behind them was Princess Ina Andrassy being squired by a tall, thin young man with a red beard. Roxanne was right, thought Paula as she spotted other well-known faces in the crowd. Everyone important is here. An audience like this is worth a million dollars in word-of-mouth publicity, if Myles doesn't flub. He won't, of course. Roxanne knows he won't, and so do Myles and Philip Rosen. Of course he's not nervous. He's played Carnegie Hall dozens of times.

She glanced at the printed program. Bach's "Goldberg Variations." No novice would have nerve enough to start a program with something that long and difficult. Then the "Hammerklavier Sonata"—who would tackle that after the "Variations" except a veteran pianist? Then the Chopin "Andante Spianato and Grande Polonaise Brilliante." After the intermission came Brahms' "Paganini Variations"; "L'Isle Joyeuse" and "Masques" by Debussy; and, as a finale, the "Mephisto Waltz." A somewhat meaty program. A Duncan Ely program, in fact.

The houselights were lowering when William de Lancre leaned over and whispered, "Mrs. Clarkson?"

Paula looked around to see the handsome stockbroker sitting directly behind her. He was formally dressed, like most of the audience.

"If you have a moment during the intermission, I'd like to speak to you."

Paula nodded. Then, as the applause started, she turned back to see her husband walk out on the stage. He made a professional bow, then seated himself at the piano. There were fifteen seconds of expectant silence as he waited for the audience's undivided attention. Then he attacked the Bach.

"You were right: your husband does play like Duncan," said William de Lancre during the intermission. They were in a corner of the crowded lobby. Behind them, the excited audience was smoking and talking volubly. It took no hypersensitivity to crowd reaction to know that Myles was a hit. The audience had given him an ovation after his masterful rendition of the Beethoven, and the flashy Chopin had brought them to their feet in a roar of approval. "And to top everything else, he's so beautiful!" gushed a nearby Young Elegants type as Paula held a cigarette for the stockbroker to light.

"Sex, style and Chopin," she said, exhaling. "I'm afraid Myles is doomed to success."

"You don't look very excited about it."

Paula shrugged.

"I'm pleased for him. But it doesn't come exactly as a surprise."

"Why?"

"You wouldn't believe me if I told you, Mr. de Lancre."

"Please call me Bill. And I'd be very interested in hearing why."

She looked at him skeptically.

"I don't like to make a fool of myself twice."

He hesitated. "About the other day: that's why I wanted to talk to you. I'm afraid I was rude to you."

"You had every right to be. I had no business asking you those questions."

"Yes, you did. And the reason I didn't answer was that I was afraid."

"Of what?"

"Of becoming involved with memories I'd just as soon forget. Namely, Roxanne. You see, I lied to you. I have seen the man in the black Derby hat."

She looked at him with renewed interest.

"Where?"

"At Saint Moritz. Twenty years ago."

"When Duncan's wife died?"

"Yes."

"Do you think he had something to do with her death?"

"I don't know." He frowned. "No, that's wrong. I *think* he had something to do with it, but I sure as hell don't know what."

"Do you know who he is?"

"No, but I can understand why he frightens you. At any rate, I think maybe if we had a talk I could ease your mind. Can I see you after the concert?"

"Roxanne's giving a party for Myles. I'll have to be there."

"Then how about tomorrow?"

Tomorrow was Sunday. It might be difficult getting out of the house.

But she had to find out what he knew.

"Do you know O. Henry's restaurant at Sixth Avenue and Fourth Street?"

"Yes. Shall we meet there?"

"At two o'clock."

The intermission bell rang. Paula stubbed out her cigarette in a sand container and started back to the auditorium. As she climbed the steps to the center doors she saw Roxanne on the opposite side of the lobby.

She was looking at her ex-husband.

Paula could tell she was furious.

All through the after-concert party at Roxanne's town house, Paula had the feeling she was being watched by her hostess.

The elegant buffet supper was a triumph for Myles. Paula thought if she heard one more of the Beautiful People gush, "You were magnificent!" to him, she would get ill. Myles was suddenly the new idol, the new "in" celebrity to be talked about, raved over and used as a private status symbol ("My dear, you mean you've never *heard* Myles Clarkson?") until he was established as a permanent fixture of New York's musical hierarchy. Then, when the whole country knew who he was, the very people who tonight were gushing over him would, with the perverse snobbery of opinion molders, turn against him ("Oh, Myles Clarkson is good, of course, but I think his play- ing's overrated"). But for the moment, he was the hero of the hour, and he took the instant acclaim with quiet self- assurance.

Roxanne came up to Paula, carrying a glass of cham- pagne.

"Wasn't it thrilling?" she said.

"Oh, yes. He played magnificently." God, she thought, I sound like all the rest of them. "Magnificently!" Talk about hackneyed!

"He's fulfilled all his promise," continued Roxanne. "I only wish my father could have heard him. He predicted this, you know. He said Myles would surprise everyone."

"He certainly surprised me, though I guess he didn't surprise you."

Roxanne sipped her champagne.

"I didn't realize you knew my ex-husband," she purred.

"I met him last week. He dropped into the Beach Bum and bought some things. I recognized him from the photos in Myles' article." (I wonder if she'll buy that lie?)

"Really? Bill picking up presents for his girlfriends? I guess he's still up to his old tricks."

"What old tricks?"

"Oh, he always has a string of rather cheap girls that he plays with. He's really rather a fool about women. That's why I divorced him, you know."

"No, I didn't know."

Roxanne smiled.

"I'm afraid fidelity isn't Bill's long suit. Did he say any- thing about me?"

"No."

"I'm surprised. He usually manages to get in a dig or two to anyone who knows me. He's really a rather vicious man, though no one believes it because of those big blue eyes and that 'sincere' Harvard accent. Take it from me, though: He's not to be trusted. I'd advise you not to have anything to do with him."

"I'm not intending to." Paula's voice was going from cool to frigid. She liked Bill de Lancre; and Roxanne's quiet assassination of his character infuriated her.

"Just the same, I'll still advise you. No, I'll go even further. I'll *warn* you."

Though she continued to smile, the tone of her voice took on an edge, and there was nothing smiling about her cold, velvet eyes. Then she went away. Paula watched her as she edged through the crowd, thinking how fantastically nervy the woman was.

She decided her jealousy of Roxanne was fast giving way to outright loathing.

The premature spring weather had vanished, and gray skies and wintry cold had returned from Canada the next day when Paula entered O. Henry's. The sawdust-floored restaurant was only half full. Its Tiffany glass chandeliers and gas lamps plunged the restaurant into a pleasant fin-desiècle gloom through which Paula saw Bill de Lancre at a small butcher block table by the wall. She joined him.

"Care for a drink?" he asked, after she was seated.

"A sherry, please. Manzanilla, if they have it."

He ordered the sherry for her and a vodka martini for himself as Paula watched him. She liked what she saw. There was something reassuring about this quiet, masculine man with the beautiful blue eyes. She realized how desperately she had missed having a man to confide in since the change had happened in Myles.

"Roxanne warned me away from you," she said. "She saw us talking in the lobby last night."

"Roxanne's not one of my greatest fans. Did she tell you I was a leering lecher?"

"Well, she didn't use quite those words. But she said you liked the ladies, and that was why she divorced you."

"I won't deny I like the ladies, but that wasn't why we got divorced. Before we get into that rather morbid subject, though, how about some lunch?"

He handed her a menu, which she glanced over.

"Excuse me," he said, "but are you wearing Shalimar?"

She smiled.

"Yes. It's my favorite perfume."

"I've never met a woman who wore Shalimar that I didn't like," he said, adding dryly, "Roxanne wears Joy."

He opened his menu. "I read your husband's reviews. They were fantastic."

"That's how I got out of the house. Myles was preening

himself-so much he decided he'd spend the whole day in bed as a reward. When I left, he was snoring."

"That's what Duncan used to do."

"What?"

"After a concert, he'd spend the whole day in bed."

The waiter brought their drinks, and Paula ordered a chicken salad, while Bill ordered a steak sandwich. When the waiter left, Bill raised his glass.

"To the man in the black Derby hat."

Paula shook her head.

"I don't think I'll drink to him, if you don't mind. Tell me about Saint Moritz."

Bill leaned forward. "When I met Roxanne, she was seventeen and I was twenty-two. I'd never seen any woman that beautiful in my life, and I fell head over heels in love. Frankly, she was in love with me, too. I asked her to marry me the fifth time I took her out, and she said yes. But there was one little thing going against the idyllic romance."

"What?"

"Dear old dad. Duncan."

"He didn't like you?"

"That's putting it mildly. He hated me. Oh, he didn't come right out and say it, but he made it pretty obvious. Whenever we were in the same room together, you could feel the hatred coming out of him like death rays."

"Why did he hate you?"

Bill leaned back and sipped his drink.

"I wasn't sure at first, and I didn't find out for almost two years. Roxanne and I honeymooned in Europe. I'm not exaggerating when I say I don't think two people could have been happier. Then Duncan and Olivia joined us at Saint Moritz for a week of skiing. Olivia was Duncan's wife. She was a nice person: warm, witty and charming. But I remember when she joined us I thought she was worried about something. She seemed nervous and moody—almost frightened—which was completely unlike her usual self."

"You didn't find out what it was she was frightened of?"

"No. She was killed the third day after they arrived. Roxanne and I were with Duncan all that day. He and Olivia had had some sort of fight—at least, I assumed they had, because they were hardly talking to each other. Anyway, Olivia was an excellent skier, better than the rest of us, and that morning she said she was going to try one of the harder runs. I had the idea she was using it as an excuse to get away from Duncan. At any rate, she took off by herself while the rest of us stuck together and went up the slope we'd been using.

"At about eleven o'clock, I remember, Roxanne and I were waiting at the top of the run when I saw Duncan looking at something on the next slope—the one Olivia was using. There were a lot of trees on it, but a trail had been cut through for skiing. There was a man walking up the trail. Duncan was watching him. And although he was more than a half mile away, I remember I was struck by the fact he was wearing a business suit and a black overcoat. I wondered why a man dressed like that would be out on the ski slopes. And I remember very distinctly that he was wearing a black Derby hat."

He paused to drink more of his martini. Then he continued.

"That afternoon, they found her body in the woods near the top of the run. You've heard about the business with the paw prints in the snow?"

"Yes. And the footprints they found around the body. Do you think they belonged to the man you saw?"

Bill hesitated.

"Yes. It doesn't make any sense, but I still believe he had something to do with Olivia's death. I'm not saying he killed her, necessarily. I mean, she was killed by an animal—"

"Did Duncan own a dog like Robin then?"

"Yes, he always had a black Labrador, and he always named them Robin."

"Do you think it might have been his dog that tore out her throat?"

Bill shook his head.

"No. He'd left the dog back in New York."

"Then was it the dog they found in the village? The rabid one?"

Bill frowned.

"I suppose it was."

"Why do you say 'suppose'?"

"Well, I saw the dog before they shot him. His left hind leg had been crippled in a trap the year before, and he had a definite limp. I saw the paw prints of the dog that killed Olivia. And though I'm no expert, it didn't look to me as if that dog had a limp. You could see in the snow that the prints of his hind legs were both the same depth."

The waiter brought their food, and they began eating. Paula found she was no longer hungry, but she took several forkfuls of the chicken salad.

"After her mother died, an odd change came over Roxanne," continued Bill. "She began to withdraw from me—very slowly and imperceptibly so that I hardly knew it was happening. But it was."

"I know what you mean," said Paula. "It's been the same way with Myles. It was so slow I didn't really realize anything was happening until suddenly—he was someone else!"

Bill nodded.

"She began to spend a lot of time with her father. We had an apartment about four blocks from his town house, and she'd walk over there during the day. I didn't even know she was going for about a month, because I'd be downtown at the office and I rarely called her during the day. But one day I caught a cold and came home early. She was gone, and when she came home she told me she'd been with Duncan. She began to grow secretive and cold. And then she got pregnant."

"Had you been planning a baby?"

"No, but I was glad it had happened. I thought it would bring us back together. But it didn't. When the baby was born, it was badly retarded." Paula felt sympathy for the look that came over his face. After a moment, he said, "Roxanne was sick, almost crazy with grief. She blamed it on me—"

"How could she? That's completely irrational!"

"That's what I thought. I found out later she was blaming me as an excuse to get rid of me."

"Why?"

"When the baby died, she moved to Reno and started divorce proceedings. I didn't contest it. And the night she moved out—she spent a few days at her father's before going to Nevada—I walked by the town house. I don't know why I did it except that I was lonely for her. Anyway, I was walking on the opposite side of the street, and I looked up to the second-floor library window. It was lighted, and I could see Duncan's head. He was sitting at his desk, and someone was standing in front of him, talking to him. It was the same man I'd seen at Saint Moritz."

For a moment, neither spoke. Then Paula said, "And you have no idea who he is?"

"Not a clue."

"Do you remember what he looked like?"

"I didn't get too good a look from across the street. But he was young."

"That's odd. He still is—I mean now, twenty years later."

"Maybe he takes vitamins, although he sure as hell didn't then. He was terrifically pale, and his eyes seemed very deep-set. I wouldn't want to meet him in a dark alley." He cut into his steak sandwich. "Well, that's all I can tell you about Mr. Derby Hat. Now you tell me something: What makes you think Roxanne is a witch?"

"Satanist."

"All right, Satanist."

She hesitated, then said, "Do you think people can kill other people by wishing it?"

"Nope. I wish I could. There's at least a half dozen people I can think of I'd wish dead right now."

"I think it *is* possible," she said, softly. "I think this man in the hat, Roxanne, Duncan, Philip Rosen, Ina Andrassy—all of them—are in some sort of Satanic cult. And I think they can work black magic."

He blinked several times.

"What gave you *that* idea?"

Paula told him. When she had finished, she said, "I suppose you think I'm crazy?"

"Well, it's pretty wild. But I don't think you're crazy. You're just scared."

"Then you don't believe it?"

"That Duncan has somehow reincarnated himself in your husband's body, and that he and Roxanne have some sort of magic oil they can kill people with?"

"Yes."

He chuckled as he finished his sandwich.

"I'm afraid I'm terribly skeptical about the supernatural."

"So am I!" exclaimed Paula. "But what else makes sense?"

"Maybe nothing's happened, and you've just let your imagination get out of hand. Just because we dream something doesn't mean it really happened. In fact, what we dream is usually a complete distortion of reality."

Paula didn't say anything for a moment.

"Maybe it is all in my mind, I don't know. Maybe it's the shock of losing Abby——"

"Why don't you try and get away for a few days? Maybe all you need is a rest."

"That wouldn't do any good. Besides, I don't know where to go."

"I'm going up to my house in Connecticut next weekend. Why don't you come up?"

She gave him a quick look. He smiled.

"We'd be chaperoned. There's an old couple who live in and watch the place for me. They're so respectable you'll gag."

She was tempted. She liked him. To her surprise, she found she liked him enormously. Talking to him had given her a sense of peace she hadn't had in what seemed like weeks.

But she shook her head. He looked disappointed.

"Why not?"

"I used to love Myles—the old Myles—and I want to love him again. Until I can find out whether this is all in my mind, or whether something really is going on. . . . Well, going to Connecticut wouldn't make me feel any better. It would be running away."

He didn't push the invitation further. The waiter started to clear the table, and Bill ordered coffee. Then he said, "Let me tell you something about Roxanne. It's something I've never told anyone else, but under the circumstances, perhaps it'll help you some way. Roxanne isn't a witch or a Satanist, or whatever you're going to call it. But she's a very sick woman."

"How do you mean, 'sick'?"

He rubbed his mouth slowly with his fingers, as if he was reluctant to say what he was thinking. Finally, he said, "You see, the reason Duncan Ely hated me was that he was in love with Roxanne."

Paula looked stunned.

"His daughter?"

He nodded.

"Crazily in love with her, and I use the word literally."

"Did she know this?"

"She found out after her mother died. That's when she

began to change. That's when she started going to his town house during the day."

"But how did you find out?"

"She told me. After the baby was born, she told me the truth. She told me the reason the baby was retarded was that its father wasn't me. Its father was Duncan."

"My God—"

"And the real reason she divorced me," he added quietly, "was that she had fallen in love with another man."

"Duncan?"

"Duncan."

A feeling of revulsion swept over her as she remembered the look in Roxanne's eyes the first night she had gone to the town house—the look of hot excitement as she watched her father playing the Schubert.

"If that's true," she said, slowly, "it explains why Duncan killed his wife, or at least arranged to kill her."

"To get Roxanne?"

She nodded.

"And it means something else."

"What?"

"He's going to kill me. For the same reason."

When she got home, Myles was sitting up in bed drinking coffee and doing the *Times* Double-Crostic. He was wearing only his pajama bottoms.

"Where've you been?"

She took off her coat.

"I want over to Sutter's and got some lunch."

"Better watch out. Their pastry can make you fat."

He seemed unusually warm and cheerful, more like the old Myles than he'd been for some time. He patted the bed next to him.

"Come over and give New York's hottest new pianist a kiss."

She was standing in the door of their small bedroom which the king-sized bed almost filled.

"I want to get a cup of tea first."

"I'll get you one in a minute. Come on. Give me a kiss."

Again, he patted the bed. She didn't want to go in the bedroom, and she didn't want him to touch her. On the other hand, as long as she stayed in the same house with

him she couldn't very well avoid him. Hesitantly, she
came in the room, draped her coat over a chair and sat
down on the side of the bed.

"I can't reach you there," he said. "Come over here by
me. I won't bite."

She put her legs on the bed and crawled across the electric blanket to his side. He put his arms around her and
pulled her down to his bare chest.

"That's better, isn't it?" He bent down and kissed her
forehead. "Now you can relax, can't you?"

"Yes, Myles," she said. He seemed so gentle, so kind,
that she did in fact begin to relax. What had seemed so
clear in the restaurant now began to muddle again.

"Why were you so tense?" he whispered as he began to
rub her breasts.

"I don't know. I'm just tired, I guess."

His strong, gentle hands massaging her, the smell of his
clean skin, the warmth of his firm body acted on her like a
drug. As his tongue darted into her ear, she closed her
eyes.

"Tired? Then that's the best reason to come to bed, isn't
it?"

"I suppose."

"Philip called. He's already got the okay for the tour.
We're leaving next Saturday for Pittsburgh, then Cleve-
land, Dayton, Cincinnati and a couple of other places I
can't remember. Anyway, we'll end up in Chicago. We'll
only be gone a week, but it'll be good experience."

"Who's 'we'?"

"Roxanne and Philip. They're going with me."

"How thoughtful of Roxanne."

"Yes, it is, isn't it? But you might look a little more excited about the tour."

She didn't say anything. He pulled her around and
pressed his mouth against hers, inserting his tongue between her lips. She pushed herself away, feeling his man-
hood pressing against her.

"Myles, not now."

"Why not?"

"Please. . . . I just don't want to. . . ."

It was a lie. She wanted him very much, but her fear
haunted her. He began unbuttoning her blouse.

"Don't tell me you don't want to."

"No, really." She wormed out of his arms and sat up, looking nervously down at her nails.

"What's the matter?"

She avoided his eyes, staring at her nails, then up at the blue and yellow wallpaper they had hung themselves the year before.

"Myles, would you like to divorce me?"

"Does it look like it, the way I'm clawing at you?"

"Seriously."

Silence. Cautiously, she turned and looked at him. His face was completely impassive.

"What makes you think I want a divorce?"

"Roxanne. I think you're in love with her, and I don't want to be in the way."

He took her hand. Involuntarily, she started to pull it away; then she gave in.

"You're afraid of me, aren't you?"

"No, of course not. Why should I be afraid of you?"

He pulled her back toward him. She didn't resist.

"Because you still have that crazy idea I'm Duncan Ely."

Her cheek was resting on his chest again, and he was continuing to unbutton her blouse.

"I don't think that anymore. Really."

A look of almost mocking amusement came into his eyes.

"I think you do."

He took off her blouse, then removed her bra. Bending down, he started kissing her bare breasts. She felt a wild, intense hunger as his lips touched her skin. Perhaps she really didn't believe it. God knows, she didn't want to believe it. How could she want a man so much if she thought he was a killer?

"About a divorce," he said as he pulled down the zipper of her skirt. "Of course I don't want to divorce you—you know that. Your problem is you can't get over being jealous of Roxanne, who's really nothing but a friend. You're the only one I've ever loved."

She wondered if he were making fun of her, but forgot it as they began to make love. She forgot everything as he thrust himself inside her, filling her with a sweetness she barely remembered existed. When they were through, she lay back. He brought her the cup of tea, which she sat up to sip. Then she lay back again and closed her eyes. He stretched his naked body beside her and began gently stroking her hair.

She drifted off into a deep sleep.

She was back in the house. The Andrew Wyeth house with the magic secret. The house that was disintegrating like Dorian Gray's portrait.

She was lying on the brass bed in the middle of the huge, empty living room. The wind was sighing through the branches of the cypress trees outside, gently puffing the torn lace curtains over the shattered windows. It was late afternoon, and a sad, gray light filled the room. For a while she lay on the bed, listening to the breeze.

Then she heard footsteps. Upstairs. The creaking of old floorboards. Someone was walking back and forth above her, in the room where Abby had been.

The footsteps headed out of the room to the landing of the stairs. She looked up and saw the man in the black Derby hat. He was standing on the landing looking at her.

"Who are you?" she asked.

"You know."

"No, I don't know! Who are you? Did you kill my daughter?"

He didn't answer.

"Did you kill Duncan's wife?"

Again no answer. The wind picked up slightly. It was a cold wind, a north wind.

"When you want me," he said, "you know how to contact me."

"I don't even know who you are, much less how to contact you! Did you kill my daughter? And why? Why did you kill her?"

He said nothing.

She heard the front door open and turned to see Myles and Roxanne come into the room. They walked over to the bed and looked down at her.

"She knows," said Myles. "She tried to make me think she doesn't, but she knows."

"What do I know?" cried Paula, trying to sit up but finding herself held back to the mattress by invisible hands. "That you're in love with your own daughter? That you're both disgusting, perverted pigs?"

They didn't seem to hear her.

"I warned her to stay away from my husband," said

Roxanne. "But she didn't listen to me. It's too bad. Now I don't think we have any choice."

"She pretends to be so moral, but she's really a little whore," said Myles. "She's probably sleeping with him."

"I wouldn't doubt it."

"That's not true!" cried Paula, but they continued to ignore her. Roxanne opened her purse and pulled out the porcelain phial. She uncorked it, then held it over Paula's forehead.

"Get away!" screamed Paula. "Get away—"

She was trying to move, but she was still held by the invisible hands. Roxanne tilted the phial, and a few drops of oil dripped out of it. As Paula felt the warm liquid splash on her skin, she saw Roxanne close her eyes as if she were praying. After a moment, she opened them again and replaced the phial in her purse.

"I'd better go now," she said to Myles.

Paula watched her husband take Roxanne in his arms and press her up against him. Roxanne rubbed his arms and shoulders as he kissed her.

"You bitch!" screamed Paula. "Get away from him! He's mine!"

Suddenly Myles was gone and the mouldering Duncan Ely was standing in his place, kissing Roxanne passionately. The repulsive sight made Paula nauseous. They turned and grinned at her: then Roxanne stepped away from her father, straightened her hair and headed for the door. Duncan paused to look down at Paula, his black-green putrefying skin and bulging eyeballs a hideous mask of death.

"How long?" he asked.

"Soon," said Roxanne. "Very soon."

They both left the room.

The oil was biting into Paula's body like a million tiny imps. "Someone wipe it off!" she screamed. "Someone wipe it off before it's too late. . . . Please. . . ."

She looked up at the landing. The man in the black Derby hat was gone. She was alone in the house with the wind, the wind which was now blowing strongly through the trees, rushing through the empty panes and gusting over her, evaporating the oil. Suddenly it died down and stopped. Then all was silence.

When she woke up, she was alone in the bedroom. She could hear Myles walking above her in the living room. The floorboards creaked slightly, and she wondered if that was what had suggested the footsteps in her dream.

After a while she slowly raised her hand to her face, almost not daring to touch her forehead. When she did, it was dry.

But, like Abby's, there was a slight slickness in the center of it.

An almost imperceptible residue of oil.

She was literally sick with fear. The force of the dream was so powerful that for the next day she had to stay in bed, too weak to do anything but drag herself to the bathroom to throw up. She lied to Myles, telling him it was just an upset stomach. She couldn't let him see she was terrified that at any moment her body would become besieged by some swift, powerful disease like Abby's body had been—that the oil was seeping through her veins and organs at that very second, perhaps, beginning the process of death, death that would be fast and irresistible. Perhaps within the next hour she would begin to feel the first symptoms, whatever they would be. A fever? A headache? Perhaps even the nausea that was keeping her in bed. Perhaps that wasn't fear, but the first sign of death. . . .

She felt like a lamb in a tiger trap, knowing that somewhere in the surrounding forest the killer was stalking her in the darkness.

She decided she had to escape.

The next afternoon she forced herself to get out of bed and dress. Trying to look cheerful, she told Myles she was going uptown. Then she caught a cab and went to the

Beach Bum North. Maggie was inside with her two assistants and a half-dozen customers. She looked surprised when Paula came up to the counter.

"Paula, what are you doing uptown?"

Paula whispered, "Maggie, can you come out and have a cup of tea with me? I have to talk to you."

Maggie looked closely at her face.

"Darling, what's wrong? You look like absolute hell."

"I feel like it."

Maggie quickly turned over the store to her girls, threw on her coat and led Paula out of the store.

"You sure you don't want something stronger than tea? It's about that time, and you look like you could use a stiff drink."

Paula nodded, and they walked up the block to a small pseudo-English pub. Once ensconced in the dark wood booth with the English hunting print on the wall, Maggie ordered a martini and Paula a sherry.

"Now: What's the matter?" asked Maggie, firmly. Her no-nonsense attitude made Paula feel better.

"Maggie, I'm scared."

"Of what?"

"Of dying."

Maggie frowned.

"Paula, what in God's name are you talking about? We're all scared of dying, but I'd say you have a few good years left. Like about fifty."

Paula shook her head.

"The same thing's going to happen to me that happened to Abby."

"Darling, that's silly—"

"It's not! Maggie, I've had the same dream! The dream I had the night before Abby died, except this time it's Myles—Myles and Roxanne—and they've poured the oil on *me!* And something horrible's going to happen to me, some disease—"

The waiter was suddenly at the table, looking at her strangely. She tried to appear cool as he set down the drinks, but her hands were trembling. After he left, she took a deep swallow of the sherry. Its nutty dryness calmed her a little.

Maggie was giving her an odd look.

"Is this 'oil' the same stuff you were talking to Myles about at the hospital?"

"Yes. Did Chuck tell you?"

"Uh-huh. Except it didn't make any sense to me. What's it all about?"

Paula explained. She told Maggie everything. And as she related it, she noticed a change come over her best friend. When she finished, she waited for Maggie to say something. There was an agonizing pause. Finally Maggie said, "Paula, would you do me a favor?"

"What?"

"Would you go see Chuck at his office tomorrow and tell him all this? I'll set up the appointment. Or maybe to-night—yes, tonight would be better. Come on back to the apartment with me now. We can have dinner, and then you can talk to Chuck."

Paula finished her sherry.

"What do you mean, 'talk'?" she asked, coolly.

Maggie gestured.

"*Tell* him all this."

"But why should I tell Chuck? I've told you. You're my best friend."

"But, darling, Chuck's a doctor—"

Paula turned cold.

"Maggie, have you been talking to Myles?"

"Myles? Of course not—"

She looked embarrassed.

"You have, haven't you? He told you about this, didn't he?"

"Now don't get excited—"

"Didn't he? Didn't he tell you I might come to you with some crazy story?"

"All right, he did." Maggie's tone was firm. "He's wor-ried about you, darling, and so am I. Now please. Chuck will know what to do. It's probably nothing but nerves or strain or something. Maybe all you need is tranquilizers."

Paula was thinking quickly. So Myles had warned Mag-gie. God knows what he'd told her—that his wife was a raving loony, probably. That means he must have told Chuck, too. Maybe they were only waiting for her to come to Chuck and tell him; then he could certify her. He and Myles and Maggie. An insane asylum. Perhaps that was the death Roxanne was planning for her: being buried alive in an asylum. She would have to lie to Maggie. Head her off to give her time. . . .

"All right, Maggie," she said, quietly. "Maybe it's a

good idea to talk to Chuck. Except not tomorrow. Make it next week. When Myles is away on his tour."

"If you think that's better—"

"I do. And promise me you won't tell Myles I told you all this. At least till after I've seen Chuck."

Maggie nodded.

"All right. Shall I set the appointment for Tuesday?"

"Yes, Tuesday. Shall we have one more drink?"

Paula sat back in the booth and said nothing while the waiter brought the second sherry. Yes, she needed a doctor, but not for her mind. For her body. She needed a complete physical checkup. That way, if there were something starting inside her . . . something caused by the oil. . . . That way she could catch it in time. . . .

A checkup. But not from Chuck. He was the enemy now. No, another doctor. A stranger. A good clinic, maybe outside New York. She could use a change of scenery. . . .

She decided to call Bill de Lancre.

After Myles had left for Kennedy the next Saturday morning, Bill picked Paula up in his yellow XK-E and started for Connecticut. It was a perfect day: cloudless and cool. The Hudson sparkled as they drove up the West Side Drive, and for the first time since her dream Paula felt her spirits begin to lift. After deciding to have the physical checkup out of town, she had asked Bill if he knew a good clinic in Connecticut. He had insisted she come to Greenwich, where one of his best friends, Dr. Mel Reynolds, ran an excellent small clinic and where, he assured her, she could be sent through on a weekend. She had agreed to stay at his house. Since her dream, she found she had an intense desire to be with Bill. She felt she would be safe with him and the need to be with someone she could trust overcame her previous reluctance to accept his invitation.

Bill owned two acres of wooded land a mile outside of Greenwich. The property looked out over Long Island Sound, and the setting, with the tree-shaded grass rolling down to the rocky beach, was peaceful and lovely. Three years before, he had built a house, commissioning a young architect out of Princeton to design it.

"Wait till you see it," he said as he turned the Jaguar.

into the gravel drive. "If you dig modern architecture at all, I think you'll fall in love with it."

A minute later, he bumped over a small ridge and turned into a clearing. Paula saw a white concrete and glass jewel set amidst the trees overlooking the Sound. Unlike many modern houses, it was tall, its glass walls, intersected with concrete bands and white steel supports, giving the impression of a soaring geometric tower. Because of the window walls, one could see the inside from the drive, and Paula noticed the interior was divided into multileveled decks, built of white wood, which spiraled up the inside walls all the way to the roof. An outside stair similarly connected two terrace decks. While the house was definitely free-form, the architect had nevertheless managed to retain a pleasing sense of unity.

"I like it," she said.

Bill nodded.

"I'm nuts about it. Come on: we'll go inside and you can meet the Bantros."

He took her suitcase and escorted her across the grass to the front door, which was opened by an elderly, gray-haired lady who resembled Maria Ouspenskaya. She was so tiny Paula thought she could be barely five feet tall. She smiled as Bill introduced her, shaking Paula's hand and leading her into the house.

"Where's George?" said Bill to Mrs. Bantro.

"Getting some logs out of the garage. The weatherman says it's going down to thirty tonight, so we thought you'd want a fire. I got a roast beef for dinner. Do you like roast beef, Mrs. Clarkson?"

"Love it," smiled Paula, wondering if the housekeeper assumed she was one of Bill's girlfriends. Whatever she thought, Mrs. Bantro gave no hint of it in her face. And after telling Bill that her husband had caught two mice in the garage, she padded off to the kitchen.

Bill took Paula into the living room, which was two stories high and dominated most of the rear of the house. The south wall was entirely glass, giving a breathtaking view of the Sound. On the west, the inner steps led up to the first deck, which gave off to a bedroom. The north wall contained a huge fireplace, in front of which were two blue sofas.

"Bill, it's fantastic," said Paula, craning her neck to look at the walnut ceiling two floors above her.

"The top floor has two more bedrooms," he said. "I'll sleep up there tonight so you can have the master bedroom. And don't worry," he added, grinning mischievously, "there's a lock on the door."

Paula smiled.

"I trust you," she said, going over to the large telescope that stood before the window wall. "I just hope Mrs. Bantro doesn't get any gloomy ideas about my moral character."

Bill lowered his voice.

"I told her you were one of my *nice* friends. She's divided all my friends into two categories: nice, and fallen women. When I bring up my fallen women, she usually burns the dinner, just to register her disapproval."

"Then I'll find out what she thinks of me when she brings in the roast beef. Oh, look: I can see Sands Point!"

She had focused the telescope on Long Island, where the powerful lens gave a sharp picture of the distant shore.

"And someone's out sailing already! Isn't it sort of early in the season?"

She sensed that Bill had come up behind her.

"Did you tell your husband where you were going this weekend?" he asked, quietly.

She straightened from the telescope.

"No. I just told him I was renting a car and driving upstate."

"And he believed you?"

"Of course not, but what could he say? After all, he's going off for a week with Roxanne. Why did you ask?"

"I just wondered."

Again, she sensed the physical attraction between them. It bothered her because she didn't want Bill to push their relationship further. At this point, she needed a friend, not a lover. On the other hand, she wondered how seriously she would fight him if he did make a pass. What a wonderful escape it would be to forget the torture of the past weeks and lose herself in the arms of this strong, kind man. She remembered Myles' galling remark in her dream and felt a twinge of embarrassment. She was no whore; but she had to admit that since she had lost her security, her need for love had increased, and she knew it would take all her will to resist Bill if he tried anything.

There was a loud barking, and a big German shepherd bounded in from the kitchen, jumped down the two steps into the living room and raced to Bill. He leaped up on his chest and started licking his face. Bill laughed as he wrestled with the dog.

"Okay, Clyde, you big ox. We know you're glad to see me."

He shoved the dog off him.

"Paula, meet Clyde. Clyde, Paula."

Paula patted the dog's head. He seemed friendly, unlike some shepherds, and wagged his tail.

"He's beautiful," she said. "Why did you name him Clyde?"

"After the movie Clyde. I wanted him to be a killer—he's supposed to be a watchdog. But would you believe I got the friendliest German shepherd in the world?"

"That's right," said an elderly man, coming in from the kitchen carrying a load of firewood. "That damned dog won't even chase the mice out of the garage. I think if a burglar got in here, Clyde would jump on him and start licking his face."

The man was George Bantro, a retired farmer who lived with his wife over the garage. After shaking Paula's hand and giving her a suspicious look, he started laying the fire in the huge hearth.

"Cold snap coming tonight," he said. "Might even get some snow. Winter's taking its time about leaving this year."

Bill drove Paula to the clinic and introduced her to Mel Reynolds, a youngish doctor whose pudginess and cigarette smoking must have been reassuring to some of his more nervous patients.

"I keep overweight on purpose," he said with a wink as he took Paula into his office. "That way, when I lecture my patients to go on diets, they don't resent it so much. Now: you want a complete overhaul, right? Any particular reason?"

"No," lied Paula. "Just a periodic checkup."

"It's a smart idea. I wish more people were as careful. Okay, let's start at A and work through to Z. If you'll step in the next room, the nurse will bring you a smock."

As Paula undressed in the adjoining room, she looked out the window at the well-kept grounds of the small clinic. In the flowerbed beneath the window, the tiny shoots of a crocus were pushing themselves up through the

earth. She wondered if she was being morbid thinking it
might be the last time she would see the miracle of spring.

It was six thirty before she was finished. Bill picked her
up at the clinic and drove her back to the house.

"You look beat," he said as she slumped into the front
seat. "Did they find any bugs?"

"They won't have the results of all the tests till Tuesday.
But he said if he were an insurance company, he wouldn't
worry about issuing me a policy."

"What did they give you? A cardiogram?"

"That was just the start. My heart's fine, at least. Then
came blood tests, and liver tests, and an encephalogram,
or whatever they call the brain test. I feel like a sieve I
had so many needles stuck in me."

"Well, I've got a bottle of La Guita sherry for you and
a good fire going, so you can relax. Mrs. Bantro is even
making a soufflé for dessert. You like soufflés, I hope?"

"I think soufflés are the nearest thing to heaven on
earth."

She curled up in the seat and closed her eyes. The sky
had clouded over during the afternoon, and the dark bil-
lows in the west suggested that Mr. Bantro's prediction of
snow might be accurate. A strong wind had sprung up,
and as Paula followed Bill from the car into the house, the
sound of the wind in the trees reminded her uncomfort-
ably of the cypress trees outside the ruined house in her
dreams. But she shook off the gloomy thought as she sank
into the soft couch by the fireplace in the living room. The
logs crackled cheerfully; and through the huge window
wall on the opposite side of the room she could see the
water of the Sound, so placid a few hours before, now becoming choppy before the northwest wind. The sight made
her feel even warmer and more comfortable, as if the play
of the elements outside intensified the warmth of the fire
within.

When Bill handed her the sherry, she smiled gratefully
and said to him, "I was wrong. Soufflés aren't the nearest
thing to heaven on earth. This fire is."

He made himself a Scotch on the rocks, then sat down
on the sofa opposite her.

"You haven't told me why you decided to take this
checkup," he said.

Her eyes were half closed as she answered him.

"More of my neuroses."

"What do you mean?"

"I had another dream."

"Our friend in the black Derby hat?"

"That's right. And Myles and Roxanne. Except this time they poured the oil on me."

"So you really think they're trying to kill you?"

She stared at the swirling flames.

"Yes, in their weird way. I'm not going to apologize anymore about my dreams. Whether they're just fantasy on my part doesn't matter anymore: I'm scared. And so—" She turned back and looked at him. The warmth of the sherry combined with the warmth of the fire to give her a feeling of blissful euphoria, which was strengthened by the sight of Bill's strong face. "And so I decided to have a checkup to see if there's anything wrong with me. You may think I'm silly, but I still feel better having done it."

"I don't think you're silly," he said.

Paula smiled.

"Thanks. I appreciate that."

He got up and put another log on the fire. Then he stood in front of the hearth.

"After what you told me last week, I did some reading on Satanism—out of curiosity, more than anything. I learned quite a bit. For instance, I had no idea it was so widespread during the Middle Ages."

"Was it? I thought it was just a few oddballs here and there."

"No, a fantastic number of people believed in it." She closed her eyes, lulled by the warmth and the sound of his voice, and only half listened as he explained how the medieval church had become so oppressive that thousands of people had come to look on it as a sort of evil, while the mirror image of Christianity, Satanism, gained the reputation of being a joyous glorification of nature and the natural, as against the condemnation of nature implicit in the church's teaching.

"In a way, Satanism was sort of like the hippie movement today," he said. "And certainly the majority of Satanists weren't evil. In fact, considering the corruption in the church at that time, I suppose a lot of them thought they were morally superior to the Christians. At least they practiced what they preached."

The log cracked and a spark popped out, hitting the screen.

"I found out something else," he continued. "Something that may make you understand Duncan and Roxanne a little better."

Now she was wide awake, listening with interest.

"Many of the witches and warlocks had familiars: cats and dogs which were supposed to be imps or devils. They gave them various names, but apparently those witches who had made a pact with the devil always gave one name in particular to their familiar. The name, in fact, was another name for Satan."

"What was it?"

"Robin. Robin Goodfellow. Robin was another name for the devil."

After a moment, he went on: "There's something else you should know. The medieval church was extraordinarily strict about whom a person could marry, as far as the laws of consanguinity were concerned. There was a good reason for it: most people lived in small communities where everyone was related to everyone else. But the problem for poor Joe Doaks in the fourteenth century was that it was very hard for him to travel anywhere. Not only did the feudal lords tie him down to his hometown, but there was also the problem of money. So on the one hand, Joe couldn't go into the next duchy to find a bride. And on the other hand, his choice in his own town was limited to the few people he wasn't related to. So a lot of young men found it really difficult to find a bride. The answer to this dilemma for many of them was Satanism."

"Why?"

"Because it encouraged incest. Whether it encouraged it to attract the Joe Doakses of the age, or whether the Joe Doakses introduced incest into the religion, I don't know. But the fact remains there was a lot of incest among Satanists. It was condoned by the religion, and of course it was one of the things the church was attacking during the witchhunts."

"Are you telling me this because you're beginning to think I wasn't so crazy about Roxanne and Duncan?"

"I'm telling you this so you can understand what they were up to. They probably were Satanists. Maybe it was the incest that got them started on it, I don't know. Maybe they were just interested in the occult. It seems everyone you meet these days is hooked on astrology or something; maybe because they think God's dead, and they're looking for something to take His place."

"Then do you think Duncan made some sort of pact with Satan?"

Bill smiled.

"You see? That's the point I'm trying to make to you. Do you think most of the practicing Christians you know make pacts with angels?"

"Of course not."

"Then why do you think Duncan could make a pact with the devil? Satanism is a religion, just like Christianity or Islam or Hinduism. There are people who believe the religion and practice its rites, just as there are Christians who believe Christianity and practice *its* rites. This doesn't mean Satan actually exists, or that you can make Faustian deals with him any more than you or I—or the Archbishop of Canterbury, for that matter—can work miracles."

"But how do you know? There *were* saints who worked miracles, weren't there? What if these people can work miracles too?"

"There are no miracles, Paula, and there's no such thing as magic."

"But I still say, how do you know?"

He smiled and shrugged.

"Let's just say you've got to have faith."

Mrs. Bantro didn't burn the roast beef. It was cooked perfectly: slightly pink and succulent.

"I guess she's decided I'm not a fallen woman," whispered Paula as the elderly housekeeper returned to the kitchen. She and Bill were seated on the upper level of the living room, which served as a dining area. Candles in handsome Georgian sticks cast a warm glow over the roast, which Bill was slicing. Beyond, in the living room, the fire spilled its cheerful glow onto the shiny oak floors where it bounced up and reflected in the huge windows.

Bill placed a Yorkshire pudding next to the slice of beef and passed the plate to Paula.

"She's a good judge of character," he said. "Do you like chutney with your beef?"

"No, thanks."

Bill poured the Nuits-St.-Georges, then cut into his meat.

"Hungry?"

"Starved. They took about a gallon of blood out of me this afternoon." She swallowed the meat, then suddenly put down her fork. Bill looked up.

"What's wrong? Too rare?"

"No: I just remembered something. The night Myles went to Duncan's house—the night Duncan died, February second—I remember he gave a pint of blood for Duncan."

"So?"

"Didn't you have to have some of the victim's blood before you could work magic?"

Bill sighed.

"Paula, I thought I'd started to convince you these people can't do voodoo."

"But the night Duncan died was the first time I noticed the change in Myles," she insisted. "So that if Duncan did take over his body, or whatever you're going to call it, then they must have needed some of Myles' blood to do it."

"They might have *thought* they were going to send old Duncan into Myles' body, and they might have used his blood to cast the spell. But casting the spell is a long way from actually making it work."

"But if they *did* do it, the real Myles is dead; and no one will ever know, because it's the perfect murder!"

"Oh, it's that, I'll grant you. As slick a killing as you could think of. But they didn't do it." He started refilling their glasses. "Although I'll admit there's a spooky coincidence about the night Duncan died."

"What?"

"Well, February second was one of the four 'holy days' of the religion. It was called Candlemas, and it was supposed to be one of the nights Satan walked the earth."

"Do you think that's just a 'coincidence'?"

He put down the wine bottle. For the first time, he didn't look quite so skeptical.

"Frankly, I don't know."

Mrs. Bantro stuck her head in from the kitchen.

"How's the roast?"

"Fine. Everything's delicious."

"Good. I'll start the soufflé. George wants to know if

you want any more firewood brought in from the garage? The storm's getting worse."

"No, I think we've got plenty. Thanks."

She disappeared back into the kitchen. Bill looked out the window, where slushy snowflakes were whirling through the air, driven by the strong wind.

"I guess the Bantros called this one right," he said, turning back to Paula. "Okay, a moratorium on spook stories for the rest of the night. Come on: eat up. Mrs. Bantro will be insulted if you don't ask for seconds."

"The oil must be some sort of perversion of the Catholic ritual," said Paula, paying no attention to his moratorium.

"What do you mean?"

"If Satanism is a mirror image of the church, then it must reverse the church's rituals. Like the Black Mass—wasn't that supposed to be the regular Mass done backwards?"

"Yes."

"Well, then, the oil must be extreme unction done backwards. I mean, when Catholics die, the priest puts oil on their foreheads and gives them the last rites. So when Satanists want to *kill* you, they do the same thing—but it's backwards! When Roxanne poured the oil on me, I remember she closed her eyes as if she were praying. She probably *was:* but she must have been reciting the regular prayers in reverse."

Bill grinned.

"Then they must have been glad when the Pope said Mass could be given in English. It must be hard as hell to remember Latin backwards."

Paula looked embarrassed.

"It's really not funny," she said.

"I'm sorry. But no more spook stories. A deal?"

"All right, a deal."

She cut into her meat, and for a while they continued to eat in silence. Then she reached for her wine and noticed he had put down his knife and fork and was watching her. From his expression, there was little question what he was thinking. She had the grace to look uncomfortable; but she was thinking the same thing.

At eleven o'clock the electricity went off.

"Damn!" said Bill as the house was plunged into a darkness that was alleviated only by the fire. "The wind must have blown down a power line."

"Maybe it'll come back on in a minute," said Paula, who was on the sofa spooning a second helping of the vanilla soufflé she had raided from the refrigerator.

"Maybe," said Bill, going to the window to look out. "But it'll probably be out till morning. And that means no heat for the rest of the night. Great!" The wind was gusting up to sixty miles an hour, bending the trees over and scraping their dead branches against the house. The snowflakes shot past the glass like white bullets. Bill turned and looked at the fire. "I'd better get some more firewood. We may have a blanket party in front of the hearth."

"You're not going out in that wind?"

"The Bantros are in bed, and I don't want to wake George up. I wish I'd had him bring in more logs at dinner."

"Oh, well, wait a while. Maybe the electricity will come back on."

Bill sat on the floor at her feet, staring into the fire. Paula watched his profile as the light danced over his smooth forehead,

"Paula," he said, "you loved the old Myles, didn't you?"

"Yes."

"What if this change in his personality is permanent?"

She thought a moment.

"I'll probably leave him."

He didn't say anything more, and she wondered if he had asked because in the back of his mind was the idea of marrying her if she left Myles. It was a new thought to her, and one that was anything but displeasing. She delighted in being with Bill, just as once she had delighted in being with Myles. Years of marriage made one forget the sheer pleasure of being with someone brand new, feeling the sensation of attraction and the fun of flirtation—for the old-fashioned word best described what was going on.

Then she thought of Myles: the real Myles. She remembered his warmth, his strength and weaknesses, the great fun they'd had together as well as the long struggle of his career. How could she forget all that? And what if he really hadn't changed? What if the "new" Myles wasn't new at all? Then what sort of wife was she, sitting in the living room of a near-stranger thinking how delightful it might be to become his wife?

It was eleven fifteen when Bill stood up and said he was going out to get some logs.

"I think the juice is off for the night, so I might as well get this over with."

He put on a sheepskin coat, took a flashlight from a drawer, then went into the kitchen. Paula picked up a copy of *Realités* and leafed through it, trying to read an article on Morocco by the flickering firelight but finally settling for looking at the photographs. Fifteen minutes passed. She put down the magazine, wondering what was taking him so long, and debated having another sherry. She had drunk more wine than she was accustomed to, and she could feel the effects of it. Deciding one more couldn't hurt her, she went to the cabinet that contained the bar and poured herself another. She took a sip and wandered to the window wall, placing her face up close to the glass and peering out into the darkness. Her breath fogged the glass; and since she could see nothing but an occasional flash of distant white which she assumed was whitecaps on the sound, she went back to the sofa. She curled up on its soft cushions, took another sip of the wine, then leaned her head back and stared sleepily at the fire. For a while she amused herself trying to make out faces in the flames. But soon she found her eyelids closing. She fought the drowsiness, then gave in to it. The delicious warmth of sleep crept over her brain and numbed her into slumber.

When she awoke, it was ten after midnight. She sat up, looking around the room.

"Bill?"

No answer. She got up from the sofa and went to the kitchen, opening the door and peering in.

Darkness.

"Bill?"

Nothing but the moaning of the wind.

Suddenly she was frightened. She remembered that a wool-lined parka hung on the back door. Bumping her way across the black kitchen, she found the coat and put it on. Then she opened the back door.

The wind whistled in, blowing a cloud of snowflakes in her face. Making sure the door was on the latch, she stepped outside and closed it. About three inches of snow had fallen, but only a light dusting remained unmelted on the ground. Once her eyes became accustomed to the darkness, the light cover of snow helped illuminate the night so that she could see fairly distinctly. The garage was about fifty feet from the house, but she saw no one near it. However, Bill's shoes had sunk into the black mud, and his prints were clearly visible leading from the back door across the large open lawn girdled with black trees toward the garage and Clyde's kennel. Lowering her head against the wind, she followed the prints, wishing she'd thought to put on boots as the slushy snow and the mud soaked into her shoes.

When she reached the garage, the prints turned to the right, heading toward the wire fence connected to the side of the garage that was Clyde's kennel. She stopped for a moment and looked around. Nothing except the gray snow and the black trees writhing against the blacker sky. Pulling the parka more tightly around her, she passed the door she assumed led upstairs to the Bantros' apartment and continued down the garage toward the kennel. As she neared the fence, she heard a strange sound. It was a whimper. Alarmed, she ran the last few feet to the end of the garage and looked through the fence.

The kennel encompassed a run perhaps fifteen feet long by ten feet wide, the north side being the end wall of the garage against which a doghouse had been built. But Clyde wasn't in the house. Though the wire gate of the run stood open, he was huddled in the southeast corner of the compound, pressed against the fence, whining and trembling. He looked at Paula but didn't come bounding out to meet her.

"Clyde, what's wrong?" she said. Then she pointed to the doghouse. "Go on. Get out of the wind." He didn't move. He continued to whine and shake, crouching in the corner, seemingly oblivious to the wind and the wide open gate. Suddenly she knew it wasn't the wind that was making him tremble.

She looked back at the ground. Outside the gate, paw marks joined Bill's foot prints in the mud, as though he'd let Clyde out for a romp. Then Bill's prints turned away from the kennel and headed back in the direction of the house. She followed them. Judging from the increased distance between them and by the fact that the toes dug much more deeply into the mud than before, he had started to run. Almost unconsciously, she imitated the prints and began to run too.

She stopped. Halfway to the house, he had fallen down. She could see where his body had skidded in the mud; she could see hand prints where he had crawled for a few feet, this time away from the house. Whatever he had seen had somehow gotten between him and the back door.

Now she was beginning to tremble, like Clyde. The dog had seen what Bill had seen; whatever it was must have been monstrous enough to terrify a German shepherd and frighten Bill de Lancre into a state of panic—and skeptical Bill was not easily frightened. Again, she stared around her.

"Bill? *Bill?*"

No answer. And no one in sight. The trees were bending, and her frightened imagination turned their bare branches into claws scratching at the sky in some frenzied rage. She debated whether she should wake up the Bantros. She was frightened alone. She felt something was standing in those writhing trees, watching her. She tried to convince herself she was being silly, but she knew she wasn't. After a moment, she ran back to the garage and rang the doorbell to the Bantros' apartment.

Nothing.

"Damn." She had forgotten about the electricity. She banged on the glass window in the door, through which she could dimly see the stairs leading up to the living quarters.

"Mr. Bantro? Mr. Bantro?"

She listened for a few moments, but apparently she hadn't awakened them.

"Oh, God. . . ." Her shoes were soaking and her feet were freezing. If only the damned wind would stop! If only Clyde would shut up!

She hurried back to the center of the yard, to the place where Bill had stumbled—or had he been pushed? No, that was impossible. There were no other prints anywhere in sight. Then what was it he had seen?

Now Bill's prints took off in a third direction toward the thin line of trees that separated the property from the beach. He was running again, even faster; at one point, he had fallen a second time, then picked himself up and kept on.

She reached the trees and stopped. She could hear the surf now, even louder than the wind, as the waves pounded the rocky beach. The trees added their eerie sound, creaking and rustling as they swayed, weirdly brought to life by the storm. Bill had run into the trees; he must be somewhere in that blackness, or beyond, on the beach.

"Bill?" she yelled at the top of her lungs. *"Bill?"*

It was useless. She debated trying to wake the Bantros again, but decided against it. It was only a short distance through the trees to the beach, perhaps twenty feet. She had to do it. She ran in, ducking her head to avoid the wildly waving branches.

Oh, God, she thought, what did he see? Where the paw prints in the mud really Clyde's? Oh, Jesus God, what was it? Where is he?

She burst out of the darkness into the relative light of the beach. Here the prints stopped, for the wind-driven spray had washed the snow from the rocks. But she didn't need the prints anymore, for now she saw him, spread out on his stomach, halfway to the water, as if he had been trying to run from the woods into the Sound and then tripped again.

"Bill!" she screamed. She ran to him, almost stumbling on the slick stones as he apparently had done. Catching her balance, she came up beside him and knelt down. His sheepskin coat was smeared with mud where he had fallen in the snow; his galoshes were caked. His right hand still gripped the flashlight, which had smashed when he fell. Gently, she touched his shoulder, but he didn't move. Then she took his arm and turned him over on his back.

When she saw his face, she felt sick.

He was dead, but his eyes were wide open, bulging from their sockets as if he had seen something unspeakable. His mouth was half open, and a trickle of saliva was still dribbling slowly over his lip. On his right forehead was a huge black lump; the skin had been pierced and good deal of blood had poured from the wound. It had already clotted. She looked down and saw the sharp rock he had fallen on. It had killed him instantly.

She stood up and backed away, beginning to sob. It was her fault he was dead. Roxanne had warned her to stay away from him, but she had disregarded her warning. Now they had killed him just as they had killed Abby and Myles, just as they would kill her, eventually. She stumbled back up the rocks into the woods, screaming as a

branch momentarily caught in her hair, pursued by her in-
coherent image of what Bill had seen as much as Bill had
been pursued by the thing itself. She pushed through the
trees back into the clearing, then ran across the snow toward the garage. The police. She didn't care if they didn't
believe her; she was going to tell them. They would arrest
Roxanne and Duncan: they had to. They had to believe
her! They *had* to! Oh, God, oh, God. . . . They'll think
I'm insane. . . . They'll laugh. . . . What can I tell them?
Some *thing* appeared out of nowhere and made a sensible,
rational stockbroker go out of his mind? But that's what
happened! *That is what happened!*

 Clyde saw something!

Oh, God. . . . But there is no God! There is only Satan.
. . . Oh, Robin-Satan-God. . . . "In the beginning Satan
created heaven and earth." . . . I am insane! I am *insane!*
What will happen to me now? Where can I go? Who can
help me?

She reached the door to the Bantros' apartment and
pounded wildly on the glass. Finally, she saw a flashlight
beam down the stairs, then jiggle as the old man hurried
down and opened the door.

"Are you drunk?" he yelled angrily.

"Drunk?" She started to laugh. "He's dead!"

"Who?"

"Bill! Down on the beach! They killed him!"

The old man rubbed the sleep from his eyes.

"You *are* drunk. Damned New Yorkers who come up
here and swill booze—"

"You stupid old man!" she howled. "Bill is *dead!* Satan
killed him! Satan came out of hell and *killed him!*"

The old man stared at her as if she were insane.

So did the police and the reporters who swarmed over
the property twenty minutes later. The electricity had
come back on, and Mrs. Bantro had taken Paula into the
kitchen and forced some coffee into her. By the time the
slightly walleyed Detective Buonfiglio had taken a look at
the body and then come into the kitchen, Paula was over
her hysteria and was even managing to talk calmly. Nevertheless, he didn't believe her.

"You mean you think he saw some ghost or something?" he asked, sitting opposite Paula at the kitchen
table and sipping the coffee Mrs. Bantro had given him.

"Not a ghost. A thing."

"What kind of a 'thing'?" he asked. She knew he was forcing himself not to laugh.

"I don't know," she snapped. "And if I knew, I'd tell you."

"A hallucination, maybe?"

"It could be. Except you saw the dog, didn't you? There must have been something real out there that scared him, because he saw it too."

Detective Buonfiglio rubbed a hairy finger over his blue double chin.

"I'll grant you something happened to the dog. But there'd be footprints if something had been out there, wouldn't there? And the only prints are yours, the dog's and Mr. de Lancre's." He turned to Mrs. Bantro. "Was he an epileptic?"

"You mean, did he have fits?"

"Yes."

"Oh, no. Mr. de Lancre was never sick."

"What about drugs? Maybe he took some acid? I've heard cases where LSD has affected people like this. Kids jumping out of windows, things like that."

Mrs. Bantro's face froze in a disapproving scowl.

"Mr. de Lancre was a gentleman," she snapped.

"Gentlemen take drugs."

"Nevertheless, *he* didn't. You can search the place if you don't believe me."

The detective turned to Paula.

"Had you two been drinking?"

"No. We had some wine with dinner, that's all. And it's ridiculous to think liquor could make you run around in circles like he did, then run down to the beach in the middle of a storm."

Detective Buonfiglio looked skeptical.

"People do ridiculous things when they're drunk."

Paula was angry.

"Bill de Lancre was *not* drunk, and he never took drugs. He was killed by my husband and his ex-wife!"

The detective squinted at her.

"Are they having an"—he wriggled his pudgy hand in a crude attempt at diplomacy—"an affair?"

"Yes."

He assumed the look of a local who had spent a lifetime hearing juicy stories about commuter morals.

"That figures. Well, were they here earlier this evening?"

"No. They're both in Pittsburgh. My husband's giving a concert there."

"Pittsburgh? Then how the hell could they have killed Mr. de Lancre?"

Paula closed her eyes wearily.

"I don't know," she sighed. "I don't know."

The detective exchanged looks with Mrs. Bantro, who gave him a surreptitious shrug. Then he got up from the table.

"Well, Mrs. Clarkson, I know you're upset about this. And of course I'll order an autopsy. We'll find out if there was anything in his system, or whether maybe he had a heart attack or something. But off hand, I'd say it looks to me like Mr. de Lancre ran down on the beach, tripped and fell on a rock. Of course, there *might* have been something that scared him—a pink elephant, maybe—"

"He was *not* drunk!"

"Well, anyway. Whatever. But far as I can see, it looks like a bad accident, period. Too bad. He was a nice man."

A nice man, thought Paula. A very nice man. Like Myles. They were both nice men. And they're both dead. They're dead so Duncan Ely can live.

And I'm the only one who can do anything about it.

Bill's mother tried to look composed the next morning when her chauffeur drove her to the house, but she was having a difficult time of it. Paula recounted to her what had happened the night before, telling the events as they

had appeared in the papers. Mrs. de Lancre listened numb-
ly, then broke down and wept. Paula did her best to
comfort her. Then the chauffeur drove her to the station
where she took the morning train back to New York. The
sun was blinking behind the racing clouds, struggling to
make the day bright, but finally giving up as the sky blan-
keted over again. Paula sat in the lurching train staring
morosely out the filthy window at the countryside. She had
a splitting headache, and she was trying not to smoke so
that the aspirin she had taken would have a chance to
work. But she felt tense, and the desire for nicotine overcame her will power. She lit a cigarette. Immediately, her
headache intensified, making her feel nauseous.

The train finally pulled into Grand Central. She lugged
her suitcase into the main concourse and made her way to
Vanderbilt Avenue, where she caught a cab. As the taxi
rolled downtown, her headache clawed at her temples till
she thought she would scream with pain. Over and over in
her mind raced the image of Bill running in terror from
something—what? Something invisible? Something planted
in his mind? Maybe it was something psychedelic, as the
detective suggested. Some hideous apparition summoned
out of his subconscious. Some primeval mental monster.
But then, why did Clyde see it too? No, the police, with a
skeptical century's need for rational explanations, could
explain away diabolical possession as drunkenness or
drug-induced hallucination. But the police didn't know
what Roxanne and Duncan were capable of. She knew.
She was convinced that whatever Bill saw had been visible,
something summoned from God knows where by her husband and Roxanne. But of course, the police had laughed
at her, as she knew they would.

She would have to fight Roxanne and Duncan by herself; she knew that now. And she knew the weapons she
would need.

The taxi deposited her in front of her house, and she
unlocked the door. The Village seemed empty on this
gray, depressing day, and the leather shop in the basement
and the antique store on the first floor had their steel gates
locked over their windows. She climbed the stairs of their
apartment, the apartment she had once loved but which
now seemed almost alien to her. Setting her suitcase in the
hall, she went into her bathroom and took two more aspirin. The headache was abating somewhat now. She came

back into her bedroom and went to Myles' bureau. Opening the top drawer, she lifted the balled socks and handkerchiefs, searching for what she hoped would be there. She found two ancient subway tokens, a mess of pennies, a half-empty roll of cherry Life Savers, but no keys. She opened the second drawer and riffled his shirts. Nothing. The bottom drawer was equally unrewarding, containing nothing but underwear, T-shirts and sweaters.

She closed the drawer and stood up, looking around the room. Where could they be? She opened the closet and felt in the pockets of the jacket she remembered he had usually worn while he was using Roxanne's town house to practice.

Empty.

She went through all his pockets. Nothing but chewing gum wrappers.

She went upstairs to the living room. She had hoped Myles would have forgotten to return Roxanne's keys to her, but apparently he hadn't. This made it more difficult. She would either have to buy a blank key, or summon up her nerve and hire a locksmith to fit a key for her. Did she dare bluff him by telling him the town house belonged to her and that she had lost her keys? Would any locksmith fall for that, with the fantastic number of housebreakings that went on in Manhattan every day? What if he didn't fall for it and called the police?

She lit another cigarette, deciding she didn't have the nerve to try it. Then how could she get in the house?

Her eyes went to the piano, the black Steinway grand that had once belonged to Duncan and that, she was convinced, he had willed to himself so he could train his new hands for the debut of his new career. The piano was piled with music. Suddenly she had an idea. Going to the piano, she searched among the stacks of music. Still finding nothing, she went around to the keyboard and looked on the music rack.

There, at the bass end, were Roxanne's keys.

She picked them up and looked at them with relief. Then she glanced down at the white and black ivories. In her mind danced the opening notes, the biting triplets of the "Mephisto Waltz." Dum dee dee, dum dee dee, dum dee dee. . . . She remembered the first night she had heard Duncan play it. On this piano, which was then in his house. With Roxanne sitting in her chair, Robin by her side, watching her father as he bewitched the music out of the strings and hammers. Dum dee dee, dum dee dee, dum dee dee. . . . The witches and satyrs twirled in their demonic dance as somewhere Satan, the Lord of the Flies, killed God and took over the universe. . . . Dum dee dee, dum dee dee, dum dee dee. . . .

Nervously, she closed the cover over the keyboard and went into the kitchen to brew some tea.

At the Dayton airport, Myles, Roxanne and Philip Rosen got off the flight from Pittsburgh where the evening before Myles had stunned his audience with his dazzling playing. It was warm in Ohio, the storm that was still clogging the New York skies having been followed by balmy springlike weather. Roxanne carried her mink over her arm as they walked into the terminal and made their way through the airport displays to the luggage pickup area. Roxanne stopped at a newsstand and paid for a New York *Times*. Then she joined Myles and Philip as they waited for the luggage to be unloaded.

"Any idea what the house will be tonight?" asked Myles.

"They think they're sold out," said Philip. "You usually get good crowds on Sunday in the Midwest."

"Look," said Roxanne. She passed the front section of the *Times* and pointed to an article headlined "Prominent Stockbroker Killed in Fall."

Myles and Philip looked at the article and nodded.

The aluminum doors cranked up, and the luggage men started swinging the suitcases from the wagon onto the racks.

It was nine o'clock when Paula got out of the taxi in front of Roxanne's town house. She tipped the cabby a quarter, for which she was thanked with a snarl. Then as the cab pulled away, she looked up and down Sixty-third Street. It was empty. Most of the houses on it were lighted, but Roxanne's was dark. Paula looked up at the empty windows. The streetlight in front of the adjacent house gleamed in the windowpanes, and she noticed they were spotlessly clean. She wondered briefly if Roxanne hired a monthly window-cleaning service.

She pulled the keys from her purse, then climbed the stairs to the front door. In the distance, a car horn blared angrily. Otherwise, Manhattan seemed unusually quiet.

She fitted one key in the lock, but it was the wrong one. She tried the next key. It turned easily, and she felt the bolt click. She opened the door and stepped into the dark foyer, closing the door softly behind her.

She pulled a flashlight from her purse and turned it on. Its beam swung around the room, passing over the two closed doors that led into the living room, then coming to rest on the stairs. She crossed to the staircase and started up. She noticed the house smelled slightly musty, which, considering that Roxanne had only been gone a day, was surprising. Perhaps the dampness from the storm had caused it.

She reached the second floor and flashed the beam up and down the corridor. It glittered like a police car as it briefly flared in the Louis Quinze mirror. A truck rumbled by in the street outside. Then, silence.

She walked down the hall to the library. The door was open, and the streetlight outside illuminated the room, casting its pale blue glow over the books. She turned off her flashlight and tiptoed into the room. As she passed the Empire desk, she looked at the tooled leather blotter on it. The Directoire lamp; the lovely Victorian silver inkwell; the letter opener with its curiously carved handle, topped by the grinning death's head. How elegantly macabre, like Duncan himself, she thought as she picked up the opener.

Going to the corner of the room, she looked through the two grilled doors that protected the collection of porcelain figurines. The streetlight didn't reach this far, but she could dimly see the porcelain phial in the center of the shelf. Carefully slipping the letter opener between the doors, she tried to pry open the small lock, but it was stronger than she had thought. Giving up, she inserted the opener to its handle and pushed it to the left. She could feel the wood springing; after a moment, there was a loud snap and the door swung open. She ran her finger over the edge of the door and was relieved to see the wood had only slightly splintered so that the break wouldn't be obvious to anyone unless he were looking for it.

Taking a small aspirin bottle from her pocketbook, she emptied the pills into the bottom of the purse, then removed the phial from the shelf and uncorked it. Carefully, she started pouring the oil into the bottle. When she had transferred about a quarter of its contents, she recorked the phial and put it back on the shelf. Then she closed the doors, pushing the lock in so they would join.

As she started toward the door of the room, she stopped, certain she had heard a noise downstairs. A soft click, as if a door were opening or shutting. Freezing, she listened for almost a minute, but heard nothing more.

A car zoomed by outside the window and she relaxed, thinking she must hurry and finish before the house shot her nerves completely. She went to the bookshelf beside the door and knelt down. There was the row of old leather-bound books. Snapping on her flashlight, she ran its beam over the titles. *Sadducismus Triumphatus* by Joseph Glanvil. *De la Démonomie des Sorciers* by Jean Bodin. *Discourse of the Subtill Practices of Devilles* by George Giffard. Jules Michelet's *Satanism and Witchcraft. Lady Alice Kyteler,* published by the Camden Society. *Illustria Miracula* by Caesar von Heisterbach. *Disquisitiones Magicae* by Del Rio. Sprenger's *Malleus Maleficarum* and *The Manuals of the Monks Inquisitors of the Fifteenth and Sixteenth Centuries.* The last volume was much smaller than the others, being no more than four inches high, and bound in elegant green leather with gold tooling. Its title, in gold Gothic letters, was *The Book of Calls,* and the top of its spine was bent over and torn in one place, as if it had been pulled out frequently from its shelf. Removing the book, she had opened it to the title page when she heard another click. Again she froze. This time the sound seemed nearer, as if it were on the stairs. She stared at the door.

Nothing.

She found she was trembling, and her forehead was damp with sweat, something that rarely happened to her. Calm, she thought. Keep calm. If this is the right book, you can be out of here in a few minutes.

She turned the flashlight on the title page and read: "The Book of Calls. Being a Compilation of Mystic Formulae and Ancient Words Made by Matthew Hopkins in the Year of Our Lord 1647. Edited by Lord Cheatham. London. 1835." She turned to the Introduction by Lord Cheatham. "These curious formulae, used by Satanists and witches in the fifteenth, sixteenth and seventeenth centuries, were collected by Matthew Hopkins, known as the Witch Finder General during the witch hunts of the 1640's. Hopkins was. . . ."

She heard something running down the hall.

She knew what it was before it came through the door.

As she stood up and backed behind a chair, she realized the clicks she had heard were the sound of nails scratching on marble floors. She raised the flashlight and aimed its beam at the door.

Robin came through.

The giant black dog's eyes blazed in the light. His jowls were curled back over his yellow teeth as, without stopping, he hurtled himself onto the chair and leaped at her throat. She screamed as his weight hit her with full force, knocking her to the floor. He sprawled on the floor beyond her, but before she could pick herself up she felt his teeth sink into her left shoulder. Snarling furiously, he tugged at the jacket of her suit as his teeth sent pain searing down her arm. She was pounding her right fist on his face, but she knew it was useless. He released her shoulder, and she tried to roll away from him; almost immediately, he was back on top of her. She felt his heavy weight on her stomach as he jumped on her; she clutched his furry throat with her left hand, holding him off as he strained toward her, jerking his head angrily to free himself. Her arm screeched with pain as his weight pushed down on it. Her right hand, which was fumbling over the carpet, found the letter opener just as she knew she could hold him no longer. Clutching its handle, she thrust it up with all her strength, plunging the blade into the dog's chest. Something resisted it for a second; it was his heart. Then she gave a final push.

The animal gurgled, then collapsed on top of her. She felt his sharp whiskers scratch her cheek as his face rolled past her onto the rug. She was sobbing with fright as she pushed his body off and scrambled to her feet. Picking up her purse, she jammed *The Book of Calls* in it and stumbled to the door. Taking a last look at the black body lying on the carpet, she hurried into the hallway and ran to the stairs. Her shoulder was throbbing; she touched her hand to her jacket and felt blood. As she ran down the stairs, she felt her head begin to ache.

She ran across the foyer to the front door, slammed it behind her and hurried down the steps to the sidewalk, where she leaned against a parked car to get her breath. As she filled her aching lungs with the cool night air, she looked up at the second floor of the house, at the clean windows reflecting the pale blue street light, the windows behind which Robin lay. For a moment, she thought the curtain was moving, as if someone had stepped back out of sight as she looked up. She wondered if there had been someone else in the house.

She heard a car coming and turned to see it was an empty cab. Running behind the parked car into the street, she hailed it.

"Hey, lady, are you hurt?" asked the bald, pudgy-faced cabby as she climbed in the back seat. He was staring at her shoulder.

"I got cut—"

"Cut? You're bleeding like a stuck pig! Want me to take you to a hospital?"

She had leaned back in the seat and closed her eyes.

"Yes, please. St. Vincent's."

"Okay. You weren't attacked or nothing? I mean, we can get a cop—"

"No, no. Just take me to St. Vincent's, please."

"Whatever you say." He started the cab. "Christ, no one's safe in this city anymore."

Her head was throbbing so intensely that she hardly felt the pain in her shoulder. I'll have to get a shot for rabies, she thought, at the same time realizing there was something ludicrous in worrying about rabies when one had nearly had one's throat torn out. The dog. The Hound of Hell. She could still smell the stench of his foul breath and feel the strength of his body as he tensed to clamp his jaws. She remembered the expression on Bill de Lancre's face as he lay on the beach, his eyes bulging out of their sockets. They would have found her like that, sprawled on the floor of the library. They would have told the police the watchdog had attacked a housebreaker, and no one would have said a thing. Another perfect murder by Duncan and Roxanne, the perfect murderers. Olivia Ely, Myles, Abby, Bill and now herself. It was infuriating to think what they had done, to think of the cool, callous way they had staged their monstrous charade, and the habitual politeness with which Roxanne pretended to be the friend and helper of Myles' career while at the same time she carried out the macabre scheme she had concocted with her father. "God sends meat, and the devil sends cooks," she had read once. Roxanne and Duncan weren't cooks: they were gourmet chefs.

Suddenly, something exploded in her head.

She felt an intense pain in her forehead, and her whole body went rigid. She started to gag.

The cabby looked back at her.

"Hey, lady, what's wrong now?"

She tried to talk, but couldn't. Her head was thrown back, and all she could make her mouth do was choke.

"Jesus Christ, she's dying!"

He pulled the cab to the curb and double-parked. Then he jumped out and opened the back door. "Are you all right?"

The rigidity had suddenly gone, and she was no longer gagging. But a new fierce pain was spreading through her skull.

"Please get me to St. Vincent's—"

She was aware she was slurring her words, and she felt a trickle of saliva run down her chin. What has happened? she thought. Oh, God, what has happened now?

The cabby took a last worried look at her, then slammed the door and got in the front seat.

She had little conception of what happened the next ten days. She was kept on drugs constantly. She vaguely remembered being deposited in the hospital by the cabby and being taken to a private room. She remembered someone saying "stroke" and wondering how she could have a stroke. Strokes happened to old people. A stroke had happened to her mother, but she had been sixty at the time. How could *she* have a stroke? She was only thirty. She remembered one day having a tube inserted in her neck. "An angiogram," someone had said. "An X ray of your brain to see where the rupture is." Rupture? What rupture?

She dimly remembered Maggie and Myles coming into her room and talking to her. Feigning the cheerfulness of hospital visitors; trying to make small talk. Myles talking about his tour and what a success it had been. Maggie talking about the Beach Bum and the land office business they were doing.

She had half-listened. When they started to leave, she managed to slur out a question.

"Am I going to die?"

She remembered the false smiles on their faces.

"Die? Of course not, darling. You'll bury us all. You'll see."

Then they were gone, leaving her alone with the nurses, the flowers and the television set that was suspended from the ceiling and that could be worked by a switch on her bed. She watched endless hours of quiz shows, soap operas, commercials, news and Johnny Carson, sleeping through most of it, then awaking to catch a few misty minutes of the endless treacle that oozed out of the tube.

Finally Chuck told her they were going to operate on her in the morning.

"What are they going to do?" she mumbled, really not caring.

He said something about putting a platinum clamp on an artery in her neck—the artery in which the aneurysm had occurred further up in her brain.

"What's an aneurysm?"

"A blowout in an artery. You hemorrhaged severely, and we had to wait till the blood clotted before we could do anything."

"Will you be able to get rid of my headache?" she asked, turning her head on the pillow and starting to go to sleep. She really didn't understand what he was talking about.

"Yes. The headache's caused by the pressure of the bloodclot. When we clear that out, you'll be okay. Dr. Schwartzman will do the surgery, and I'll be assisting."

Surgery: an ugly word. It smelled of death. She wondered what it felt like to die. She had read once that it was supposed to be like falling asleep.

Perhaps that wouldn't be so bad.

She remembered nothing of the operation except an intense coldness which she was told later was caused when they packed her in ice to lower her body temperature and pulse while they opened her skull. The operation took six hours. She didn't come out of the anesthesia until the next morning.

Her first sensation was that the headache was gone.

Her second sensation was a clarity of thought she hadn't had since she stumbled out of the town house, however many days ago that had been.

Her third sensation was seeing Chuck standing by her bed.

"How do you feel?" he said.

"The headache's gone." She noticed she still had a little

difficulty talking, though she wasn't slurring her words as before.

"You had a little more than a headache. Can you raise your right arm?"

Surprised at the question, she lifted her arm slowly.

"Move your fingers."

She obeyed. She found that her fourth and fifth fingers barely moved at all.

"Okay. Put your arm back down."

She lowered her arm. Chuck pulled up a chair and sat down.

"I guess I don't have to tell you you've been pretty sick," he said. "But first, can you tell me where in the hell you had been the night they brought you in? Your shoulder looked like it had been chewed."

Now it was coming back to her. Robin. The attack.

"I fell down the stairs at home," she said, still not trusting Chuck enough to tell him the truth. "I guess it tore open my skin."

"You guess? Don't you remember?"

"No. Something happened just before I fell."

"You must have had the hemorrhage at the top of the stairs and blacked out. At any rate, we were able to tie off the artery and remove the clotted blood. So chances are you'll be okay in, say, six months."

She turned her head on the pillow.

"Why six months?"

"Well, the hemorrhage was on the left side of your brain, which has caused some paralysis on the right side of your body. Your speech has been affected slightly, though it's a lot better now, and as you saw, you're having some difficulty working your fingers. It could have been a helluva lot worse than it is. You're a pretty lucky lady."

"Real lucky." Paralysis! Again, she tried to move her fingers. They only partially obeyed her mental command.

"We have a regular physiotherapy program for this sort of thing. Daily massage and special exercises, and you ought to be as good as new in six months."

She closed her eyes.

"Does this happen to people my age often?"

"It can. You can be born with an aneurysm and never have the slightest clue it's there until one day, bang. It pops. It usually happens when you're older, though."

"My mother died of a stroke. Do you think I inherited a tendency for them?"

"That's hard to say."

"Can I have another one?"

He didn't answer for a moment. When he did, she noticed a note of caution in his voice.

"Well, it *can*. But it's unlikely." She heard him move his chair back as he stood up. Then she felt his hand take hers and squeeze it. "You're going to be okay, Paula. Don't worry. Now you'd better get some sleep."

As he headed for the door, she said, "The irony is I just had a complete checkup the day before this happened."

"I know," said Chuck, at the door. "Dr. Reynolds sent the results to Myles. He said there wasn't a thing wrong with you."

He left the room and closed the door.

Myles visited her every day, several times coming with Roxanne. They both were pleasant, chatting aimlessly, telling her she looked better, encouraging her. Neither of them once mentioned Robin, which Paula couldn't understand. Surely they had found the dog's body, noticed the broken lock on the bookshelf door and concluded someone had broken in? Surely they would have guessed it was probably she who had done it? But either they didn't know, or for some reason they were pretending they didn't. Neither alternative made much sense.

Unless He was helping her. It was a new thought, but as she mulled it over she began to see it might well be the truth. And if it were, it put things in a different light. A more advantageous light.

She pulled *The Book of Calls* from her purse and began rereading it.

She turned the idea over in her mind at least a hundred times. It frightened her, but the alternative frightened her more. For the alternative was death. She had no illusions about Roxanne now; she and Myles had killed four others to get what they wanted, and they would kill again. She had only delayed it by managing to stab Robin; Chuck had only delayed it by the operation. Perhaps they would wait until she was out of the hospital before another aneurysm would rupture, or an artery would clog. They had a thousand ways to kill her, and they would do it.

So as frightening as the idea was, it was less frightening than the alternative.

Maggie came to visit her. She looked troubled. She handed a bouquet of anemones to the nurse, then leaned over the bed and kissed Paula.

"You look better," she said.

"I feel better."

She sat down next to the bed.

"Chuck says they're going to start the physiotherapy tomorrow. He says you're going to be as good as new before long."

"Maybe," said Paula, wishing she could share Chuck's optimism. "How's the store?"

"I sent one of my girls to run the Bleecker Street place. She's doing okay. Business is a little slow this week. Tax time's coming up, and people are getting chintzy."

The nurse came back in the room with a vase in which she placed the anemones. Filling it with water in the bathroom, she brought them over for Paula to see.

"Aren't they pretty?" she asked.

"Yes, they are. I love anemones."

"Where do you want them?"

"Put them on the windowsill. That way they'll get some sun."

The nurse placed the vase in front of the window where the blues and reds of the flowers were bathed in the bright sunshine. Then she left.

"I think I ought to tell you something," said Maggie. "Unless you don't feel up to bad news?"

"I wouldn't know how to take good news. What's wrong?"

"Well, you've been here almost two weeks now. And—" She frowned. "Hell, I hate to be Old Mother Snoop, but I think you ought to know what's going on between Myles and Roxanne."

Paula didn't look surprised.

"While the cat's away, the mice do play, don't they?"

"I could be wrong, but, well, I dropped by your place the other night to see if Myles wanted to come over for dinner and a movie. She was there."

"Did Myles at least look embarrassed?"

"Not a bit. Cool as a cucumber. And Myra Schulman told me she went to see *Joe Egg* last week, and who was sitting in the eighth row on the aisle?"

"Huntley and Brinkley?"

"Roxanne Huntley and Myles Brinkley. I mean, apparently they're not even trying to hide it! It's just made me furious. I never dreamed Myles was like that."

Paula stared at the ceiling.

"He wasn't. This man isn't Myles."

Maggie looked at her.

"Paula, you still don't believe that crazy story you told me? About Duncan Ely playing musical bodies with Myles, or whatever?"

Paula shook her head slowly.

"No, I don't believe it. Maggie, would you do me a favor?"

"Of course, darling."

"You and Chuck have a good lawyer, don't you?"

"Yes, Garry Sutton. He drinks like a fish, but he's still a good lawyer."

"Would you get him to come see me?"

Maggie raised her eyebrows.

"Are you thinking about a divorce?"

"In a manner of speaking. I want to make a will."

"A *will?*"

Paula sighed.

"I know: I'm going to live fifty years, and I mustn't be morbid and think I'm dying, and everything's going to be hunky-dory. But I've had one stroke, Maggie, and I may have another. At any time. So I want to make out a will. And, Maggie?"

"Yes?"

"I'm leaving my half of the Beach Bum to you and Chuck."

Maggie looked stunned.

"But what about Myles—"

Paula turned her head and looked at her.

"What about him?" she said flatly.

Maggie said nothing. She got up and took Paula's hand.

"All right. I never fight being mentioned in wills, even if I know I'll never live to inherit it—"

"Oh, Maggie, spare me the cheery bedside manner!" snapped Paula. "Don't you see what they're doing? They're killing me! Don't you *see* it? Do you think Abby *really* had meningitis, or that Bill de Lancre just flipped his lid that night? For God's sake, open your eyes! I'm *not* crazy! Myles and Roxanne are murderers. They've got one more person to get out of the way, and then they're home free—and that person is me. And the damned thing about it is, no one is ever going to be able to prove they did it."

Maggie stared at her with disbelief.

"But, darling, if that's true, why don't you tell the police?"

Paula sighed.

"I did. They laughed at me, just the way you do. Besides, what could they do even if they did believe me?"

The nurse came back in the room.

"Lunchtime, Mrs. Clarkson. I'm afraid visiting time is up."

Maggie nodded.

"All right."

"A big treat today, Mrs. Clarkson. Doctor says you can go on a regular diet. We've got chicken a la king, and something yummy for dessert."

"What?"

The nurse beamed.

"Devil's food cake!"

Paula managed to curb her enthusiasm.

The lights in the rooms were turned out at ten o'clock.

Paula lay in her bed thinking about her childhood. She didn't know why, but she kept thinking of her tenth birthday party. Her father was alive then, and he had only begun his long and agonizing descent into drunkenness. She remembered he gave her a bicycle, and how thrilled she had been with the present. Then all of her friends coming in for the party. The ice cream and cake. The eleven candles—"One to grow on," he had told her as she filled her lungs to blow them out. "One to grow on." To grow to what? To grow to this night. The most important night of her life.

At midnight she got out of bed. She was weak and walked with difficulty, her right leg being stiff. Holding on to the furniture, she limped to the door and quietly shut it. Then she went to the bathroom door and pushed it further open. The light spilled out into the hospital room, illuminating the darkness.

She limped to the window and looked out. Four floors below her, the city spread out in all its garish splendor, while above it a gibbous moon glowed in a clear, ebony sky and the blinking red light of a jet eased itself down toward Kennedy. Across the street the marquee of the Loew's Sheridan Theatre was dark and the last customers were straggling out after having seen *Guess Who's Coming to Dinner*. She looked at all this; then she limped to the bed and pulled the aspirin bottle and *The Book of Calls* from under the blanket.

She knelt on the floor by the bed and uncapped the bottle. Carefully, she poured the oil on the floor in the shape of a pentagram. In the center of the figure she traced a cross. Then she damped her index finger in the oil and touched it to the center of her forehead, her ears, her eyelids, the tip of her nose and finally her lips. Then she made the sign of the cross in reverse.

"I shall have no other gods before me but Thee, O Master," she whispered, reading from *The Book of Calls*.

Again, she traced the cross on her chest.

"I shall go wherever Thou commandest, O Master, and shall do Thy biddings."

Again, the cross.

"Ie n'ay rien qui ne soit a toy, en ton nom Seigneur cette tienne seruante s'oingt, et dois estre quelque iour Diable et maling Esprit comme toy. Venez, O Antecessor. Venez, venez, O Diable. Venez, Prince et Pere. Venez, Dieu."

She closed the book and sat, kneeling, waiting.

For a few moments, all was still. Then she heard footsteps coming down the hall. They grew louder: then they stopped.

She watched the door, waiting hopefully for it to open.

Part IV

1

She was released from the hospital three weeks later.

She had made remarkable progress with the physiotherapy, and while she still limped and there was yet stiffness in her fingers, her speech was practically back to normal. Chuck was enthusiastic. "You've done much better than I ever hoped," he said as he and Myles helped her into a taxi. "Maybe I was pessimistic when I said six months. We'll stick to the time schedule—no use getting our hopes up too soon—but still I'm really very pleased with the way things have gone."

Paula kissed him.

"Thanks, Chuck. You've been wonderful to me. I really appreciate it."

She climbed in the back seat of the cab.

As they drove down Seventh Avenue, she looked at her husband sitting next to her. Now that she knew the truth, she was no longer afraid of him. She was even surprised to find her old love of him had started to rekindle, despite his obvious disinterest in her. She had found she was looking forward to his visits to the hospital, even though they were so patently forced, and when he would come into her room she would feel an excitement, the same excitement she used to feel, so long ago before it had all started, when she would be near the old Myles. It was a sexual excite-

ment, for she still desired him, and her long hospitaliza-
tion had only intensified the desire. She was amazed she
could still feel such hunger for a man who, after all, was
responsible for the death of her daughter and who would
be responsible for her own death. But she couldn't deny
the feeling, though she was rather ashamed of it. She
wanted Myles' body, even though the soul was another
man's. And she intended to have it.

He helped her up the stairs of their house. It was difficult for her, but Chuck had said that climbing the stairs
would be good exercise for her as long as she went slowly.
When she finally reached the top, she felt relieved being
back in her own home. She went into the bedroom and sat
down on the bed, smiling at Myles.

"It's good to be back. I was getting awfully tired of that
hospital."

He nodded.

"It's good to have you back. Can I get you anything?
Like some coffee?"

"No, thanks. I'll just sit here for a while and get my
breath. Then I'll unpack. I don't want you to worry about
me."

He forced a smile. She knew he was trying to think of
something warm to say, some little sign of happiness at
her return. But of course he couldn't, since naturally this
was a day he had been dreading.

She decided to take him off the hook.

"Don't you have to be at the studio pretty soon?"

He checked his watch.

"I'm supposed to be there at eleven."

"Then you'd better go." He looked relieved. "What are
you recording today?"

"The four Chopin scherzi."

"Sounds like a good day's work. When will you be
home?"

"Oh, probably around five, maybe later. It all depends
how the recording goes. I'll call you to see how you're
doing."

"No, don't bother. I'll be fine. Don't worry about me."

He shrugged.

"Well, you've got my number if you need me. If you're
sure you're okay, I'd better run."

"Aren't you going to kiss me?"

He looked slightly guilty as he came over to the bed and kissed her. She ran her fingers lightly over his strong jawline, then rubbed his cheek affectionately. What beautiful skin he had! What marvelous eyes, what a superb nose, what a magnificent mouth! She wanted to hold him, to embrace him, to never let him go. She would hold him; but not now. There was a better way to do it.

"Good-bye, Myles. And good luck with the record."

"Good-bye."

Still looking rather guilty, he hurried down the stairs out of the house.

She sat on the bed awhile, thinking of Abby. He had explained why Abby had been killed: it was part of the contract. A child sacrifice, He had said. It was a horrifyingly high price, but one they had been glad to pay. Now she was going to pay a high price too; but though it would be unpleasant, it was nowhere near what they had had to pay. She was thankful for that.

She stood up and limped over to the chair where Myles had placed her suitcase. Opening it, she ran her hand under the neatly folded nightgowns. Her fingers closed over a small bottle which she pulled out. Its label was marked $CHCl_3$. *Chloroform*. Reaching back into the suitcase, she fished out the other object she had stolen from the hospital.

It was a hypodermic needle.

She placed the bottle and the needle in her largest purse, adding some wads of cotton and a small bottle of alcohol. Then she slowly climbed the stairs to the living room and went to the piano. She looked at the floor: there were the electronic pitch-finder and the tuning wrench. She leaned over and picked up the wrench. Its wooden handle and solid steel head were perfect for what she needed. Besides, there was a nice touch of irony, under the circumstances, in turning a tool that tuned pianos into an instrument of revenge.

Returning to the bedroom, she wrapped the head of the wrench in a handkerchief, then placed it carefully in the pocketbook with the bottle and the needle.

Dabbing some Shalimar on her ears and throat, she brushed her hair, frowned at her haggard reflection and put on her coat. Then she picked up the phone and dialed Roxanne's number.

When the cab let her off on East Sixty-third Street, she noticed the Rolls-Royce was parked in front of the town house. She limped to the gleaming fender of the car and looked up and down the sidewalk. Except for two pedestrians near Park, the street was empty. She pulled the tuning wrench from her purse, and took another look around to make sure no one was watching, and slammed the tool with all her strength against the car's headlight. There was the crash of shattering glass. Picking two shards of glass from the handkerchief, she replaced the wrench in her purse and calmly hobbled up the steps to the front door and rang.

After a moment, Bennet opened the door.

"Is Mrs. de Lancre in?" asked Paula.

"As I told you on the phone, Mrs. Clarkson, she's still in bed."

"Would you tell her I have a book and some oil to return to her? I think she'll want to see me."

The butler indecisively opened the door to let her in.

"Very well. Will you wait in the living room, please?"

He opened the two tall doors, and Paula entered the large room with its starkly modern decor and its huge op art paintings. She looked at the piano at the end of the room, the twin to the piano in her own home. She remembered the night they had first come. She and Myles—the old Myles. With Duncan playing the "Mephisto Waltz." That had been the beginning.

A few minutes later Bennet returned.

"Mrs. de Lancre will be down as soon as she gets dressed," he said.

"Thank you. Oh, Bennet, isn't that Mrs. de Lancre's car parked in front of the house?"

"Yes?"

"Someone seems to have smashed the headlight."

Bennet looked annoyed. "I suppose it's some of those idiot teen-agers. . . . Thank you, Mrs. Clarkson. I'd better take it to the garage. Will you tell Mrs. de Lancre?"

"I'd be glad to."

From the window, she watched Bennet hurry out of the house, look at the smashed headlight, shake his head with disgust, then get in the car and drive away. Looking satisfied, Paula left the window and went to a chair. The house was silent. She opened her purse and pulled out a pack of cigarettes, which Chuck had told her she must stop smoking. Poor Chuck. He was taking such pains to prolong the life-span of her body, when there really wasn't any point to it at all. Inserting a cigarette in her holder, she leaned back in the chair to wait.

After a while, she heard footsteps in the hall, and Roxanne came into the room. She was wearing a green silk peignoir which flowed loosely down from her shoulders, giving her the appearance of a classic goddess. Closing the double doors behind her, she looked coolly at Paula.

"Bennet said you had some oil to return to me. What oil?"

"The oil I stole from the phial, of course."

Her face became suspicious.

"Stole? When?"

"The night I had my stroke, when you and Myles were in Ohio. I used Myles' key and got in the house." She placed the cigarette in an ashtray, then stood up and started limping slowly toward Roxanne, who seemed confused.

"How did you get the phial?"

"I pried the doors open."

"But you couldn't have! I'd have noticed—"

"He fixed them for me. He fixed everything because He wanted to help me."

Now Roxanne looked startled. Paula quietly clicked open her purse.

"Bennet helped you? I don't believe it."

"I didn't mean Bennet. *He* helped me, because He wants to collect you."

"What *are* you talking about?"

"Really, Roxanne, there's no point in playing games anymore. I know everything. He told me, and He's made a contract with me: you for me. You've been free a long time, so you don't have much to complain about, wouldn't you say?"

For an instant, Paula was sure Roxanne was lowering her mask. There was a look of uncertainty in her eyes—uncertainty mixed with fear. Then the mask returned. "I think you're out of your mind," she snapped. "Now get out of here before I call Bennet."

Paula shrugged.

"Call him."

As Roxanne went to the doors, Paula pulled the wrench from her purse, stepped up behind her and brought it sharply down on the back of her head. Roxanne grunted softly and fell to the floor.

Her eyes were closed, but Paula knew the blow, softened as it was by the handkerchief, had only stunned her. Taking the chloroform out of her purse, she unwrapped the handkerchief from the head of the wrench, soaked it with the anesthetic, then kneeled down and held it over Roxanne's nose. She twitched once or twice, then lay still and began breathing deeply. Paula removed the handkerchief.

Reaching into her purse again, she took out the cotton, the alcohol and the hypodermic; then she rolled up the sleeve of the green peignoir and located a vein in Roxanne's right elbow. Dipping a wad of cotton in the alcohol, she cleaned the needle, pushed the air out of it, and rubbed the vein with the disinfectant. Her hand was trembling as she kneeled down and placed the needle against the soft skin, but she didn't hesitate. Firmly, she pierced the flesh and the vein. Then she began to draw the plunger back.

The clean glass tube slowly filled with dark blood.

When it was full, she pulled the needle out and placed a fresh wad of cotton on the puncture. Replacing the hypodermic, the cotton and the alcohol in her purse, she picked up the tuning wrench and the handkerchief and looked down at Roxanne. She was sleeping peacefully.

Paula opened the doors and looked into the foyer. It was empty, and the house was still. Quietly, she stepped out and closed the doors behind her. Then, moving as quickly as she could, she headed for the stairs and started to pull herself up. When she reached the top, she limped down the corridor to the library.

She was relieved to find that what she needed was still hanging on the wall.

2

It was two thirty in the afternoon when Maggie climbed the steps to the small foyer of Paula's house and rang her bell. Her arms were filled with an immense bunch of white chrysanthemums she had bought as a welcome-home present for her friend, and the flowers almost covered her face. She peered over them to nod to Messrs. Random and House, whose shop door was open because of the pleasant weather.

"We're certainly glad Paula's out of the hospital," said Random.

"Yes, it was a terrible thing that happened to her—simply terrible," added House, who enjoyed talking about other people's illnesses. "But we're glad she's back."

"We're all glad," said Maggie.

A middle-aged matron with her teenie-bop daughter sailed through the door to look at the "sweet" French chair in the window, and Maggie watched with amusement as Random began his understated sales pitch. Then she rang the bell again.

After almost five minutes, she began to wonder what was taking Paula so long. She knew she was slow on the stairs, but it certainly wouldn't take her five minutes to come down to open the door. She signaled to House, who came out of the shop.

"Paula is home, isn't she?"

"Oh, yes. She went out this morning, but she came back —oh, at least an hour ago. Why? Doesn't she answer?"

"No. Maybe she's taking a nap. May I use your phone?"

"Sure, but we have a key. Why don't I just unlock the door for you?"

Explaining that Paula left a spare key in the antique store in case she lost or forgot her own, he unlocked the door, and Maggie climbed the narrow stairs to the second floor. She looked in the bedroom; the bed was rumpled, but the room was empty.

"Paula?" she called.

Nothing.

She decided House must not have seen her go back out, and she went into the bathroom to leave the flowers in the tub. She'd go home, then drop back in an hour or so when Paula would have returned.

The bathroom floor was wet, and the flowers prevented her from seeing what was in the bathtub until she was at its edge. When she did see, her scream was heard not only downstairs in the antique shop but in the leather shop in the basement as well.

"Why in Christ's name did she do it?" whispered Chuck twenty minutes later as he stood beside Maggie, staring down at the tub. It was filled to the brim with water that had turned almost completely red. Beneath the faucet, which was dripping slowly, he could see the top of Paula's head a few inches below the surface, her hair floating lazily around it like a golden aureole. Her naked body drifted on the bottom, and though the water was almost opaque from the blood, he could see the deep gashes in her wrists and the razor blade that had made them.

"I think I know," said Maggie, who had stopped crying although her eyes were still red. "See that mask over her face?"

Chuck leaned closer to look at the white object.

"It's a mask of Roxanne. And see this?"

She pointed to a water glass on the floor by the tub. It was empty, but its sides were coated dark red. Beside it was the hypodermic needle. Chuck picked up the glass and inspected it.

"Blood," he said. "What in the hell was she doing?"

"I think she drank it."

"*Drank* it?"

"Remember that crazy idea she had about Duncan Ely taking over Myles' body? She told me she thought Roxanne had made a life mask of Myles because they needed a mask to work the spell."

Chuck stared at the mask of Roxanne again.

"You mean Paula thought she could put her soul into Roxanne's body?"

Maggie nodded.

"Not only that—I'll bet Myles and Roxanne *convinced* her she could."

"Why?"

"Oh, Chuck, don't be thick! You know they've been sleeping together while Paula was sick. They probably planned this ages ago, planting all this Satanism crap in her mind and making her actually *believe* it to the point where she kills herself, thinking she's going to float uptown and be Roxanne from now on. At which point, dear old Myles and Roxanne have it made."

"Christ, Maggie, that's murder!"

"Of course it's murder!" she snapped, bitterly. "The slickest and sickest murder anyone's ever dreamed of! Both of them ought to be hung from the nearest lamppost! But of course they're going to get away with it. Who could prove it?"

Chuck looked down at the naked body dangling grotesquely in the red water, pickled in death.

"Maybe she was depressed about the stroke."

"Oh, come on! Depressed? So she puts a mask over her face and drinks blood? That's hardly the usual way people fight depression. No, she believed it. She believed it so much that she didn't mind killing herself. Look: see that book in the tub by her feet?"

She kneeled down, rolled up her sleeve and dipped her arm into the still-tepid water to fish out the small, green book with the gold Gothic title. She held it over the tub as the water dripped off it, then opened it. "See? *The Book of Calls.* She probably was saying this mumbo-jumbo as she slit her wrists, the poor kid. God, I'd love to tell the police about Myles and Roxanne, even if they can't do anything to them—the bastards."

"Well, you're not."

"Why not? They shouldn't be allowed to waltz off scot-free."

"For the simple reason that it wouldn't be fair to Paula. The newspapers and TV get hold of this and they'll have a field day. 'Housewife Kills Self in Pagan Orgy'—the whole bit, which won't do anyone any good, including us. Particularly since she willed us her half of the Beach Bum. If I thought the cops could do something, I'd say okay. But as it is—"

Maggie sighed.

"I suppose you're right." She was silent for a moment. "Then maybe we should get this stuff out of here before you call the police. I mean the mask and the hypo."

"Shouldn't we give them to Myles?"

Maggie took a bath towel off the rack and started placing the objects in it. "And let him and Roxanne have the satisfaction of knowing their bitchy little scheme worked? To hell with that. Let them keep guessing."

She reached back in the water and carefully lifted the mask off Paula's face. As she pulled it out of the water, she let it drip for a moment, then placed it on the towel with the book and the needle. Folding the corners, she made a bundle out of it and put it under her arm. "You call the police," she said to Chuck, "and I'll take these things home."

Chuck nodded and went into the bedroom. Maggie took a last look at her friend, then followed him. She hurried into the hall and down the stairs to the foyer, where Random and House met her.

"Is anything the matter?" said House, anxiously.

"She's dead," said Maggie, leaving them gaping as she hurried down the steps to the sidewalk. There were a number of shoppers out, lured by the beautiful weather. She weaved her way through them, the towel under her arm, until she reached the corner of Sixth Avenue. As she waited for the light, she noticed a young man in a black suit watching her. He came up and politely tipped his black Derby hat.

"Pardon me. You're Mrs. van Arsdale, I believe?" He spoke with a soft voice and an Oxford accent.

"Yes—"

He looked at the towel.

"Ah, I see you've got the mask. I was coming to pick it up, but you can have it. It doesn't matter now."

As Maggie stared at him, he nodded and started on.

"Who are you?" she asked.

He turned. There was an amused expression on his face. "My name's Bill Grainger," he said. "I work for Philip Rosen. I'm in publicity."

He walked away and disappeared in the crowd.

Myles arrived at Roxanne's town house at ten after six that evening. He let himself in with his key, slammed the door and ran to the stair.

"Roxanne!" he called.

He waited impatiently until she appeared at the top of the stairs.

"I've got some good news."

She started slowly down the steps, her hand lightly grasping the banister, her movements graceful and sensuous. She was wearing white lace hostess pajamas that clung tightly to her superb figure. The top had a deep neckline with a high collar that showed her beautiful breasts in all their snowy glory; her black hair was pulled back in a chignon, and her face was perfectly made up. She had never looked more haunting.

When she reached the bottom of the stairs, he took her in his arms and put his mouth up to her ear.

"I'm a widower," he whispered with a grin.

Her face remained impassive.

"Did she have another stroke?"

"No. She got in the tub and slashed her wrists. Don't ask me why. Maybe she was scared, I don't know. Anyway, she's dead—finally. I'd say this calls for a drink."

Roxanne ran her fingers through his hair.

"Don't you think you should display a little guilt? After all, she was your loving wife."

Myles laughed. "She was a dull little hausfrau," he said. Then he dug his mouth into her neck and started kissing her, slowly rubbing his hands over her back. Roxanne closed her eyes and said nothing.

After a moment, he looked up. He seemed puzzled.

"You've got on something new."

"I know."

"Isn't that Shalimar?"

Roxanne smoothed her hair back, then took his hand. Smiling, she led him toward the living room.

"Come on, darling. Let's have that drink."